LETHAL SHADOW

JB TREPAGNIER

500 YEARS AGO

For once, I wasn't the youngest person in the room. The other mistresses in the room were younger than my twenty-five years, but they were all human, unlike me. In five years, they'd all be trying expensive creams to look younger while I was still desperately hoping for more life experience.

I was immortal, unlike everyone at this dinner, and a hybrid to boot. I was an infant compared to the other supes, and I was thousands of years younger than the very first hybrid, Aria Emanuele, but there still weren't many of us out there. Some supes thought we were special, with a purpose, and some still thought we were abominations. Those that thought we were abominations would never say that out loud. Aria's father was king of all supes and would give the final death for that.

I may still be an infant to my kind, but my parents seemed to think I was ready for this mission. My mother was a vampire warrior, and my father was a warlock diplomat. Pretty much, both of them were against the idea of hybrids until my father was sent on a diplomatic mission to my mother's court to send spies to investigate the rising Ottoman empire.

My mother actually looked down on warlocks, and my father thought vampires were filthy bloodsuckers. They antagonized each other for months before realizing they liked giving each other a hard time. My father went to hex my mother right when she went to bite him in the middle of an argument. They were both wanting to kiss each other, and it sealed their fate as mates.

Hybrid births were hard on both mother and baby. Sometimes, the mother didn't make it, or the baby was stillborn. There was the issue that you had a single natured mother trying to grow a dual-natured baby. My mother said she ate like a horse, needed more blood, and required a lot of magical herbs when she was pregnant with me. She swore she had an easier time with me than other mothers because she wasn't a witch drinking blood, she was a vampire drinking witch tea.

My mother wanted me to be a warrior like her. *I* wanted to be a warrior like her. I wanted to be like Aria, the first hybrid. No one told Aria what to do. I was good with the sword, and I was taught to fight, but I was definitely my father's daughter. As much as I wanted to be this fierce warrior, I was merely competent. I could defend myself perfectly fine. No one would ever be able to hurt me, but it was my school lessons, I excelled at.

My parents met over the rise of the Ottoman Empire, and once I was old enough, I was undercover working higher-ups with that government. Between my vampire nature and my witch nature, I could find out any secret. I could make people do whatever I want. I could compel like a vampire without eye contact.

I wasn't just a vampire witch hybrid. Witches and

warlocks descended from twins who had a falling out. One twin had eyes that glowed silver and was stronger with manipulation. The other twin had eyes that glowed gold when she was casting magic. She was gifted with writing her own spells.

Before the territory wars, it was unheard of for a silver-eyed witch to mix with a witch with gold-eyed witch. It still wasn't common now. The falling out between the twins still carried down to the covens now. The gold-eyed covens found the silver-eyed coven's magic dirty because it lay mostly in manipulation.

Not only was I the daughter of a vampire and a warlock, but my grandmother was a gold-eyed witch, and my grandfather was a silver-eyed warlock. My father's eyes glowed gold when he was using magic, but not me. My pupils glowed red because of my vampire blood, and then I had an inner ring of silver and an outer ring of gold.

I hated it the first time I saw it in the mirror when I was a child. I thought it would get me killed. My father had a tutor work with me. This wasn't supposed to be possible among witches and warlocks, but my tutor taught me how to make my eyes stay hazel when I was using magic.

It served me well in the six months I'd be undercover at this huge palace trying to find out what these humans were up to. Humans were so confusing. I was here as a mistress instead of a warrior or diplomat. That was apparently all women were good for according to humans. Sex and making babies. They didn't even let them vote.

Being alone with my mark was easy. I'd just compel him to sit across the room and tell me what I needed to know, and then I'd put a sleep spell on him where he'd fall asleep thinking we'd had sex. Being at these dinners with him was awful. These men wanted pretty, silly women. They didn't want us to have opinions. They wanted us to sit there, look pretty, and laugh at their jokes. It went against everything in me to just sit there, giggle, and flutter my eyelashes.

No one reported to me there would be a raid. I wasn't listening for heartbeats because these dinners were boring and uneventful. There were also armed guards everywhere. Everyone inside should have been safe. The villa we were in wasn't in the city. It was way out in the country.

My vampire hearing heard the cannons before they started bursting through the walls. I would have exposed myself, but I fully intended to use my vampire speed to get the hell out of there. I stood up among the chaos and rubble and realized the guards that were supposed to be protecting us had surrounded the table and were killing people. I hadn't even pushed my chair back when pain ripped through my abdomen. I looked down and saw the point of a Yataghan poking through my dress.

I'd never felt pain like that before. I needed to feed before I passed out from blood loss, but some of these men had the new arms the Ottomans were using. No one was quite sure how to kill hybrids yet, but there were theories. If I grabbed the man who stabbed me to feed, one of them could shoot me in the head. I had no idea if that was fatal.

Still, I needed to get out of here. Blood was pouring out of the gaping wound in my stomach. Maybe I could get him under the table and bite him there. I managed to turn around, but I was starting to get dizzy. The man who stabbed me looked surprised I was still standing. I couldn't get to him in time, and he ran me through again.

I collapsed on the floor. I could smell smoke. The villa was on fire. I had to find a way out of here before I was burned. I was holding on to consciousness by a thread, but I could sense something new in the room. I felt magic being used. The room went deathly silent.

Two strong arms picked me up and cradled me to a hard chest. I was looking at a huge, blonde warlock with ice blue eyes and long hair.

"I've got you, Liliana. You're safe now."

I had no idea who he was, but he made me feel safe. I couldn't fight it anymore. I passed out.

500 YEARS AGO

I had no idea where I was when I woke up or how long I'd slept. I woke up in a huge bed in an ornate castle I'd never been in before. The same blond warlock who took me away from the burning villa was sitting on a chair next to my bed watching me sleep. I knew I hadn't had blood, but my wounds weren't a sore as they should have been.

The blonde warlock jumped up when he saw I was awake. "I've healed your wounds as best I can, but I know you need blood," he said, craning his neck.

I'd never fed from the neck before. I'd never been allowed. My father always said it was too intimate and I should always feed from the wrist until I met my mate. This warlock had to be one of the most handsome men I had ever seen. He had huge blue eyes framed by long lashes, and he wore his long blonde hair tied back. He had this perfectly straight nose and a full mouth. He was giving me this easy-going grin like it was totally fine for me to bite his neck and he had this dimple in his cheek I wanted to touch.

"Who are you?" I asked. Most supes didn't offer blood. Vampires fed off humans unless you were mated or lovers or you had a vampire child. When I was a child, I was given blood from the wrist of prisoners in my mother's dungeon. I still only fed off humans and never supes. We had a dungeon full of human criminals for our blood needs. I had no idea why this warlock wanted me to bite him. Wasn't it too intimate for him? Or didn't he consider me dirty for drinking blood?

"Explanations can wait, Liliana. You aren't totally healed. Your aura is still weak. Perhaps you'd prefer to feed from someone else here? I want you to get to know me, and you can do that if you bite me."

He was right. I could tell a lot about him from his blood, but I didn't think I could bite his neck just yet. I hadn't even had sex yet and I just couldn't. This warlock was probably much older than me and wouldn't understand a virgin baby hybrid being uncomfortable at a little neck bite.

"Your wrist," I said, managing to pull myself into a sitting position. My wounds weren't as sensitive, but I was still weak from losing blood, and I did need to feed. I was expecting him to get judgey, but he just gave me this easy-going grin. He sat next to me on the bed and offered his wrist. Not only was he beautiful, but he also smelled good.

"Have you been bitten by a vampire before?" I asked, hesitating.

"When they needed healing, sure."

Who was this warlock, anyway? A wave of dizziness hit me again, and I couldn't put this off. I sank my fangs in his wrist and shuddered as his blood hit my throat. I felt a connection to this warlock with my fangs in his wrist. His blood was rich, like some dessert. I could tell he had a lot of secrets, but I also knew he was willing to share them with me. Was he my mate?

I didn't want to remove my fangs when I'd taken enough blood to heal. I wanted to shove him on his back and have him be my first lover, but as soon as I let go of his wrist, he went back to his chair. I'd never had a crush or been in love before. Was this what it was like? I wanted him back in bed with me, and I didn't even know his name or where I was.

"Liliana, what I'm about to tell you is top secret. If you agree, you will be warded to never speak of it. If you don't, your memory will be wiped, so you don't remember. We've had our eye on you for a very long time. We need you."

I sighed. He was too good to be true. He clearly wasn't my mate. He wanted to use me.

"What exactly do you need a hybrid for?" I asked, slumping my shoulders. I didn't care how attractive I thought he was, and I probably wasn't going to do what he wanted. I still didn't know his name or who *we* meant, but if he thought he could manipulate me into doing something just because I was so young, he was wrong.

His blue eyes looked surprised. "We don't need a hybrid. You would have been brought here if you were just a witch or warlock. You're here because Godfrey reported you're smart as hell and talented. You don't need to be going on diplomatic missions telling other people how to run countries. *You* need to be running countries."

"Who are you, anyway? If you hurt Godfrey, I'll break your neck and drain you dry," I growled. Godfrey had been my tutor since I was a child and he wouldn't betray my family or me. If he told this warlock anything about me, it was under duress. But why hadn't my parents recalled me to tell me Godfrey was missing?

"Your eyes are quite unusual and rather lovely when you are holding magic. Godfrey told me, but it's startling in person. Godfrey is perfectly safe and still with your parents. Can you put your magic away and hear me out? You've had my blood, and I think you know I mean you no harm."

I was so confused. His blood told me he was safe and didn't want to hurt me at all, but he had intel on me he shouldn't, and he wanted me for something. I released any magic I was holding and leaned back into the pillows. It would take a little while before his blood totally healed me so that I couldn't attack him right now anyway. But once I was at full strength, I wouldn't hesitate to rip his head off if I was here for something bad.

"Godfrey prepared you for this in his own way, when he realized how special you were," he said softly. He finally didn't have that smile on his face like everything was easy for him. "Do you remember the stories he used to tell you in your gardens when you did well in your lessons?"

"He told me supe myths and legends. They were just stories. He told them to me because I wanted to be a fighter, like Aria, but I was better at school work."

"Ah, but he prepped you to be a fighter in your own way. The Order of the Red Shadow is not a myth; we just make damned sure everyone thinks that. You're at our headquarters, and I'm *trying* to recruit you without you hexing me or draining my blood."

I thought this was huge prank someone was playing on me. I'd agree to join, and then I'd be a laughing stock when I got back home — the baby hybrid who still believed in bedtime stories. This warlock had to be pretty stupid to try to embarrass me considering who my mother was. Something wasn't right.

I'd trained for this. No one, not even a warlock, could keep secrets from me. Godfrey had taught me how to hide my eyes from glowing when I was using magic, but I didn't bother this time. I wanted this warlock to know he was under my control. My vampire blood flowed through me faster, and my heart rate always sped up when I used my vampire abilities with magic.

The warlock in front of me went totally stiff and was under my compulsion now. No spell existed for him to fight this. Whatever he told me now was the truth.

"What is your end game? Why am I really here?"

"The Order of the Red Shadow is a tribunal, but we have spies and assassins too. Godfrey is a member. We put Order members close to every new hybrid because we know they are in danger from other supes, even now. It was Godfrey that reported you would be good for The Order. Humans are expanding and starting wars. Some of these wars, we know a warlock is responsible.

"Godfrey suggested you. Our spies and assassins try to end wars, and when we do, another government takes over that could be just as bad. The Order has been watching you. Someone with your skills could control several countries at once, setting people in place for a government that is for peace, not war. You could help us root out this warlock we've been hunting."

I let my magic go, and he collapsed in his chair panting. He still gave me that grin like he thought everything was going to work out. I was still in shock all the stories I was told were actually true, and they wanted me of all supes to be a part of it. And run entire countries at that.

"Do you see why we want you? I was nineteen when the territory wars ended. You know how old that makes me. You're only twenty-five, and I was totally powerless against you. You're amazing, Liliana, and if you join us, you will do great things."

"Who are you and where am I?" I demanded. I still didn't know his name.

"Ah, we went straight for secrets instead of the basics. My manners have failed me. My name is Xenon Drabek, and you are in Requiem Coven territory in the Swiss Alps. We moved The Order headquarters here after Piero's death. Raffaele was a young king when the territory wars happened, and Piero never wanted him in The Order.

"We made a huge show of being against Raffaele's punishment so that we could have privacy here and because we were hoping the true coven responsible behind the territory wars would confide in us. They haven't, and we suspect whoever it was is the warlock responsible for the wars we keep having to end. We have suspects, but no proof."

I knew nothing about Xenon. All I knew about Requiem was that they wanted to be left alone. Now, I knew why. Could I do what they thought I could do? Juggle several countries and stop a coven that set things in motion thousands of years before I was born? I wanted to. The fact that both Godfrey and Xenon believed in me lifted me up. I wouldn't be arm candy to some piggish politician trying to get information for my parents until humans finally decided women were worth more than sex and making babies. I could make *real* change.

"I do want to join you, but not without further training and education. You know how young I am."

"Great!" Xenon said, his grin widening. "Once you're up to it, come to meet everyone, and we'll have a celebration feast for our new member. My mate was concerned for you when she found out about the attack on the villa, and she's been dying to meet you."

Xenon had a mate? Of course, he did. He was thousands of years old and would have found her by now. That didn't mean he didn't interest me and I wasn't attracted to him. I'd just have to keep it to myself until I happened to find mine. It didn't matter the species; mates were territorial. I remembered my mother biting a new tutor because she thought the woman was giving my father the eye.

I had no idea if Xenon's mate was a witch or another species, but I didn't want to be on the receiving end of the mate wrath of any species. I could pretend I wasn't interested in Xenon, but there was this blooming curiosity there that I already knew was going to get me into trouble.

5 YEARS AGO

If you had told me when I was twenty-five and agreed to join the Order that hundreds of years later, I'd be running several countries from behind the scenes, I would have thought you were crazy. I ran most of Europe until a new face showed up on the scene. His name was Zimin, and he showed up almost out of nowhere during elections. We all watched as all the politicians under my compulsion lost and Zimin took over Russia.

My hold on Russia slipped, and Zimin was impossible to get close to. We already knew he had supernatural help. No one had an astronomic rise to power from nothing like that without magical help. It was just so far, every time someone like Zimin came to power, and another war started, the asshole witch or warlock helping them was careful.

I was still young for a supe. I was only a little over five-hundred-years-old, but I wasn't the shy twenty-five-year-old Xenon pulled from a villa after being stabbed. I stayed in the Alps for a hundred years being trained by various supes before I started running countries.

That little seven-year-old that always wanted to wield a sword like her mother or another weapon, like her idol, Aria Emanuele, didn't need a physical weapon. Xenon and coven members from all over the country trained me in all sorts of battle magic. Godfrey and a few other vampires taught me how to use my vampire abilities to fight.

My compulsion skills and spell writing ability were honed, and before I was sent out, Xenon wanted me to pick bodyguards because back then, it was almost unheard of for an unmarried woman to be alone on the street. If someone came after me, I'd expose myself fighting them. Humans were burning other humans as witches. They'd probably burn a real witch for once if they saw what I could do.

I was flat out shocked at all the volunteers for my bodyguards. It was just naturally accepted that I would have a sip of their blood as part of the interview. As part vampire, it was how I would know I could trust them with my life. Nearly every species of supe came forward to meet me, some that were even rare then and now.

Some of them just wanted the glory of guarding a hybrid. Some just thought it would be an easy job being set up in posh villas while I ran things in the background. Some had seen me training and hoped guarding me would lead to us being lovers. There were also several good spies and assassins that put their name forth because they just wanted to protect me and thought my job was important.

It was hard to choose. I settled on a Lycan, a Fae, an Incubus, and a dragon shifter. Quinn was a Lycan from the Shadowtooth pack in Wales. I picked him because he was one of my victims during training. He taught me how to defend myself against a Lycan and never complained when I blasted him on his ass. When he could stand up, his wolf would be peeking out in his amber eyes, but he would just keep going until I'd mastered what I was being taught. I could trust Quinn and Quinn knew exactly what I was capable of. Quinn was huge, like all the Lycans and roped with muscle, but I already knew if it came down to it, he wouldn't view me as a helpless woman.

The Fae were normally a snooty bunch who thought they were superior to other supes, but Cirrus was pretty low key. He was from Scotland with shocking red hair he wore long to cover his pointy ears and sparkling green eyes. While I had my fangs in his wrist to get a taste of his blood, he swore he would teach me to celebrate victories like an honorary member of the Fae. Cirrus was also deadly with his staff, and I'd noticed him watching when I was being taught to fight with one. Cirrus wanted this job because he respected how hard I tried when I was learning the staff.

Colnar, the Incubus, I still don't know if I picked him because his blood told me I could trust him and I knew he was a fierce warrior, or he was sending sexual energy to me with his blood. He'd never tried using his Incubus abilities with me, and he was always discreet when he needed to feed. I never regretted picking him. Having an Incubus on your team turned out to be handy now that women were being put in positions of power. He could feed, get information, and make a kill look natural if needed.

Jago was my dragon and rounded out my team. I think I was just so excited to meet one, I would have picked him without biting him. Dragons were *extremely* rare, even before humans started hunting them. Dragons could only have children with their mates, and it had to be done in dragon form. The female had to stay a dragon the entire time to produce an egg. A child with harden scales came out of the egg, but the entire process for dragons to mate and have children involved being in their dragon form for extended periods.

This was already hard before humans. There were so few dragons; it was hard to find a mate. Dragons cared about their mates, their children, and their treasure. They guarded those three things above all else. When the covens were made human, long after humans had forgotten this, they discovered dragons and their trea- sure. It didn't take long to figure out the vulnerable spot on their hide. They were killing pregnant mothers, and male dragons were dying of hunger trying to protect their mates.

I wasn't a mate, a child, or treasure, but I knew from Jago's blood he would protect me like I was. And hell, he was a fucking dragon. He could half shift where he looked like a human, but had his dragonhide, or he could go full dragon and take out entire buildings.

I was proud of my team. We worked well together over the hundreds of years we had been working together. We had a good working relationship. They were all much older than me and probably thought of me like their kid sister. If I hadn't been in love with Xenon since I was twenty-five knowing full well he was mated and I could never have him, it would just make sense for me to date one of them.

I didn't even try. I did date, and it always ended in disaster because I couldn't get over my hang-ups over

Xenon. I didn't even want to try with my bodyguards to see if they could get me over that warlock because I didn't want to change how things were between all of us. If only had I known.

Xenon showed up at my villa in Russia out of the blue. That always threw me for a loop. Everything I thought I'd let go of being so far away from him would just come flooding back in. It didn't last long this time. He gave us a mission. He wanted me to run against Zimin and put myself in the public eye. An easy glamour would disguise my appearance, but if there was a warlock close to him, he would sit up and take notice of a hybrid with four supe bodyguards.

I was surprised Jago, Cirrus, Quinn, and Colnar were against it. They spoke out and thought it was a stupid idea. I frowned. They knew what I was capable of. I was an assassin in my own right now. Sometimes, if someone was resisting my compulsion too much, I'd just kill them and glamour myself to look like them.

They had no way of knowing what was going to happen to all of us any more than I did.

5 YEARS AGO

Asking Nature for something must be like asking for a curse. As I competed against Zimin for power in Russia, I heard more from Xenon. I was supposed to give a speech, and I needed to nail it. That morning, I put myself into a trance to commune with Nature. I asked her to get rid of my feelings for Xenon. I didn't ask for a mate or a relationship. I just wanted to move on.

After the speech, where I had rallied everyone there to support me, we went back to my villa. I stopped outside the gate. I could feel a strong hum of magic. I held my hand up.

"Something is wrong. Someone breached my wards. It was a human, but I feel magic."

Cirrus tapped his magical pen, and his staff exploded out. "There's a—"

We had no time to react or run. We were all thrown backward as a huge blue explosion rocked my villa. My back slammed into a tree fifty yards away, and I was fighting consciousness. Jago stood in front of me, dripping blood. His skin was beautiful, iridescent green and gold scales and his eyes were totally golden with a cat-like green slit down the middle.

"Check on the others," I groaned as he checked me for injuries. For some reason, it was very important to me that they were okay, even though my entire body was aching and I was pretty sure everything was broken.

"Sorry, Liliana, you're my priority. Out of everyone here, I'm the least injured. We aren't alone. I can sense metal nearby — guns and steel. We need to get out of here. Think you can cloak a dragon?" Jago asked, heaving me over his shoulder.

I was weak, but I thought I could. He set me next to Quinn, who looked like his body was twisted worse than mine. He offered me his wrist. I'd fed from the neck now with my unsuspecting lovers, but never from my bodyguards.

"No," I said, placing his wrist back on his check. "You need your blood."

I could tell his back was broken. Since he was Lycan, it would heal with food and sleep, but I hated seeing him like that. I placed my hands over him and let my healing magic go into him. He tried to fight me, but he was too hurt.

"No, Liliana! Your leg is broken, and you need blood. Take my blood! Just a little, okay?"

I listened for heartbeats trying to clear the fog in my head. If we had been any closer to the magic bomb, we would all be dead. Jago came back with Cirrus, who was totally unconscious. Jago set Cirrus next to me, and he would have been able to hear me and Quinn's conversation.

"Take a little of his blood," he whispered. "All of us

are going to need you to heal us, and we may need to fight. The metals are getting closer, and I can hear their thoughts. They are under orders to shoot on sight and bring the bodies back to Zimin's place."

I nodded. "Please, go get Colnar so we can get out of here."

I listened to heartbeats. There were five humans and six warlocks with odd heartbeats. I knew that heartbeat. Sorrow Leaves. If anti-drug commercials for little witch children were a thing five hundred years ago, I would have been forced to watch them. My father taught me about Sorrow Leaves, and The Order trained me on them later.

Sorrow Leaves were a plant that used to be rampant during the territory wars — a weed that used to kill crops. Some of the less savory witches and warlocks used it for all sorts of things. If crushed and smoked in a pipe, it could be used as a temporary power boost, but was extremely addicting and had side effects like human meth.

I was taught it was used in the curses on the land to start the territory wars. It was outlawed, and it was supposed to be extinct now. Someone must have kept seeds and was growing it in secret like human marijuana.

These warlocks had to be linked to Zimin, and all of us were too weak to fight. I withdrew my fangs from Quinn's wrist. His back was healed, so I started using my healing light on Cirrus. Where the hell was Jago with Colnar?

"Can you smell them?" I asked Quinn.

"Too much blood and that magic bomb is too strong. We need to get out of here and get it a healer. Eventually, the magic we absorbed from that bomb is going to start affecting us. They wanted us alive, or they would have set it off when we were inside, not outside."

I nodded and sighed with relief when Jago came back with Colnar. We were a sorry bunch. We all had broken bones except Jago, and I was starting to feel the dark magic from the bomb creeping its way through my veins. When I looked down my hands were starting to spider with black lines.

"Jago, can you get us to the Raven's Nest Coven? They are close by and friends. We need to get there *fast*."

Jago lay flat on his back. "Climb on top of me and hold on tight. Liliana, if you can, cloak me. Charred warlock is my favorite snack, but these wankers will have to wait."

I managed to drag my broken body across Jago's. "You can't eat them anyway. They've taken Sorrow Leaves. You'll get sick."

"That damned virus," he growled, his body starting to mutate. The Sorrow Leaves had been ground and put into spiced wine that started this huge supe virus that caused vomiting and skin lesions. The Order was pretty sure whoever planted the wine hoped it would be fatal, but apparently, it was just more of an annoyance. The Order narrowed it down to the wine and got it off the street.

It was top secret that Sorrow Leaves *were* fatal to hybrids. I didn't know that until I joined the Order. Xenon and the others had no idea if they were fatal to me since I was half witch, but I was always told to steer clear of them. Even if we weren't all bloodied and broken, I couldn't have bitten any of those warlocks.

I'd never seen Jago go full dragon. Quinn trusted me with his wolf, but there was never the appropriate time or space for Jago to change. I'd seen him with golden eyes and his dragon armor, but here I was not only getting to see his dragon, but I was also getting to ride him, and I couldn't even enjoy it.

My body was screaming in pain, and my skin was turning gray from the magic in the bomb. I'd only taken a little blood from Quinn. Just enough to try to help the others. I'd lost quite a lot of blood myself, and my vision was turning red.

I hardly noticed the huge, gold and green wings start beating next to me and all of us start lifting off the ground. Jago wasn't immediately going to Raven's Nest, and I was wondering what the magic bomb had done to him. I was holding on with everything I had to keep him cloaked, and I had no idea why he was flying back to my ruined villa instead of Raven's Nest territory, which was in the other direction.

I could see small bodies on the ground: men in Zimin's red uniform and warlocks in black cloaks. Jago swooped down, and this infernal orange flame came out his snout. All the men went up in flames in seconds, and Jago finally changed directions towards Raven's Nest territory.

"The warlocks were out, but blackened human is also a nice treat. Everyone hang on tight. It's going to be a rough flight, and I can already tell that the bomb is affecting me. Liliana, can you reach out to Raven's Nest so they can prepare for us and possibly a rough landing?" Jago said in my head.

I gritted my teeth. Holding onto a dragon with a broken leg while communing with a coven *and* trying to cloak all of us? I'd been trained for working through pain. I just had to do this and try not to pass out.

Sybil was my contact in Raven's Nest. I reached out

to her with my mind and hoped she was awake. Sybil kept strange hours, even for someone who was dating a Satyr.

"Liliana, darling? You feel wretched. How did someone manage to get the hex over on you?"

"Magic bomb at my villa. We're all injured and hexed. Do you have someplace Jago can land? He's feeling the hex, and it may be a rough one."

"Jago let you ride on his back? Liliana, dragons just do not let anyone mount their backs. Do you know what this means?" Sybil was squealing and sounded excited about something. I had no idea what it was, and it wasn't the time.

"It means he's doing his job and keeping our team safe. I've got Cirrus, Quinn, and Colnar with me. We're going to need a good bit of healers when we get there and someone to remove the hexes. I can tell it's more than one."

"Aim for the bank of the Tura Basin. We'll be waiting."

I relayed that information to Jago and checked in with Quinn and Colnar behind me. Quinn was going feral and struggling with his wolf. It wouldn't do to have a feral Lycan behind us hundreds of feet in the air on the back of a dragon. Colnar groaned.

"I can try to fix it, but it may not work on him, and if it does, he's got every right to punch me if we ever get to the ground," he yelled.

"Just do it," Quinn yelled.

Now, I was on the back of a dragon, with a broken leg, a half-feral Lycan, and an Incubus sending out sexual energy to all of us. If I weren't in so much pain and trying not to pass out, I would have laughed I was now getting horny on top of everything. I'd never taken up with an Incubus before, and Colnar kept his sexual energy reined in around us before. If I wasn't about to pass out from blood loss before, I was about to now from the energy Colnar was sending out. Couldn't he just aim it at Quinn and leave the rest of us out of it?

The snarling and growling from behind me was starting to lessen, and Colnar pulled his energy back. I took a step back from the growing grayness of my skin to wonder how Quinn could even be affected by an Incubus. He was a hot-blooded Lycan who flirted with anything in a skirt. I guess he had grown out of that because he stopped doing it over the last hundred years or so when we went out, but it was definitely curious.

It was summer in Russia, but my body temperature suddenly dropped like it was the middle of winter. My entire body started shaking, and I needed to figure out what this hex was. Gray skin and feeling freezing cold? Quinn was having issues with his wolf? It sounded like some custom written hex. We needed to get to the Tura Basin soon.

I could tell we were following the Tura River, and it wouldn't be long, but Jago was starting to fly like a human drunk driver. I could see the basin and where we would land, but I didn't think we were going to make it. I hardly had any healing light left, and I desperately needed blood, but I started sending it to Jago. I hoped it made it through his armor.

"Jago?" I called, hoping he could still hear me. Quinn's wolf nearly took over. I didn't know if Jago's dragon was in control.

"I'm holding on, love. I'm trying to get us to land."

We were so close. I could see witches, warlocks, and several vehicles waiting for us in the distance.

Jago let out this unreal shriek and the next thing I knew, the huge dragon I was holding onto disappeared.

Jago was back in his human form, and we were all plummeting towards the Tura River Basin. I tried to conjure a bubble of magic to shield us, but my magic wasn't coming. My body felt ice cold, and my stomach was in my feet from the feel of falling.

My last thought as my body slammed into the river and my vision went black was that no one knew how to kill a hybrid and there was mostly only one way to kill my bodyguards and friends.

But could we die from drowning?

5 YEARS AGO

The stories told to little supes when they were children was that if you were bad, you'd end up in Tartarus for eternal torture. Later, you'd be taught if you weren't bad enough for Tartarus, but you weren't good enough for Elysium, you'd end up in Asphodel Meadows.

The last thing I remembered was the magic bomb and plummeting towards the Tura River. I had no idea where I was. All I could see was pitch black, and something was pulling me in four different directions, but I could not go anywhere. Sometimes, there was this intense peace that would wash over me, and I'd get a respite from the waves of pain that kept washing over my body. I'd never felt pain like this.

I was sure I was in Tartarus, but for the life of me, I had no idea how I ended up there. Was joining the Order the wrong thing? Every time I tried to think, intense pain would overtake my body. I was starving, and I wanted blood, but there was no one here to drink from. I could feel something close that went in four different directions, that I *needed* to get to. Whatever was pulling me towards it could save me, but I couldn't get to it.

It seemed like I fought for days. Whatever was waiting for me, if I could just get to one, I could get to the others. I had no idea what was pulling me, I just knew I desperately needed to get to it. My salvation was in four different directions. I didn't question that. I just fought to get to it.

It seemed like this had gone on for months when I heard whispers of voices. If I concentrated hard enough, I could pick one out. It was a voice I knew, and I just didn't know how. I knew that voice had meaning to me once, but getting to whatever was pulling me towards it now was more important than that voice ever was.

I was starting to feel things now. The pain that came in waves finally stopped, and it was almost like I was alive again. I saw a pin of light. Maybe that light could get me to whatever I was struggling so hard to get to. The voices were clearer now.

"Did you see that? Her finger moved!" I felt a hand stroking my face. I had a face? Was I not dead? "Come back to us, Liliana. The worst is over."

That voice again. I knew that voice. If I had a face to touch, then I had eyes, and I wasn't dead. I struggled to open my eyes. I think I got them open, then immediately shut them again. There was some sort of harsh light above where I was that hurt my head.

Even if I wasn't dead, whatever was pulling me while I was in whatever dream state, I had been in was so close. I needed to get out of this bed and find out what it was. I struggled to sit up, but it was like my body was made from lead. I felt hands pressing on my shoulders.

"Can someone shut the lights out and light candles?

Liliana? Are you back? You scared the shit out of all of us. You need blood. Please, open your eyes and drink. The lights are off."

My eyes fluttered open. There was a blond warlock in front of me. Xenon was here. He must have come when he heard I was injured. Before I fell in the lake, that would have sent my stomach in a mess of butterflies, but I felt nothing. I'd had Xenon's blood before. I had it when I first met him, and he'd given it to me to recover when he was training me.

I had no idea what was going on with me. I thought of Xenon fondly, but only as a friend now. And for some reason, I couldn't take his blood right now. I needed it, and my throat was parched, but it just felt wrong to drink his blood, even for healing. The blood I needed, craved, that felt right, was in four different directions, just like when I was passed out.

I listened for heartbeats. A dragon, a Lycan, an Incubus, and a Fae were pulling me towards them. My team? Were they as bad off as I was and why did I want to go to them so badly? Why did I feel like it was wrong to drink Xenon's blood when before that magic bomb exploded, he was my first and only love?

"The hex?" I managed to croak. This was clearly part of the hex. Once Xenon and Sybil managed to fix me, everything would go back to normal.

Xenon sighed. Sybil was also hovering over me poking me with her magic. "The hex is totally gone. It was a tricky one. Custom written for every single one of you meant to disrupt your connection with Nature. We managed to figure it out while all of you were passed out and reverse it. Do you feel any different?"

"The hex is still there. Quinn, Jago, Colnar, and Cirrus, they did something to us."

Xenon and Sybil exchanged glances like they were hiding something from me. I heard crashes from outside my door. I heard all four of them yelling and fighting to get in. I let out the breath I was holding. They were alive and out of bed. And I *needed* them in here with me for some reason.

They needed me too. Whatever this hex was, it was pulling them to me as strongly as it was pulling me to them. They were practically trying to break the door down and yelling they knew I was awake. They apparently just *felt* it.

"Let them in. Please," I begged. "Then, you can figure out how to break the hex."

Xenon smoothed my hair off my forehead. Not just a few days ago or however long ago I'd passed out, that gesture would have sent shivers through my entire body. Now, I just felt nothing. Xenon always had this easygoing smile on his face, but he looked pained right that minute.

"Liliana, the hex is gone. Somehow, the assassination attempt and how you all worked together to get here marked all four of them as *your mates*. What you're feeling isn't a hex from the bomb. You're feeling the mate-pull of four mates at once, and they are trying to break the door down because they are feeling it too. If I let them in here, they may kill each other. We need to keep you apart until we figure out what this means."

"No," I croaked. My throat felt like sandpaper, and the only reason I hadn't started to dry out was that I was half witch. "Blood." It was getting harder and harder to talk.

Sybil nodded like she understood what Xenon couldn't. "She doesn't want *your* blood. She only wants the blood of her mates. You might think it's a good idea to keep them apart and you're probably right, but now that Liliana is feeling the mate-pull, she's only going to want the blood of her mates."

Xenon sighed. "I'll go talk to them to minimize any mate drama when they get in here hopefully. Liliana, drink from *all* of them, so no one gets jealous and find an order for them that doesn't start any fights."

I still thought this was part of the hex. People just didn't get four mates like this. It was just a recipe for supes killing each other. Once you felt the mate-pull, this fierce, protective urge overtook you until you marked your mate and even after you marked them, jealousy was always going to be an issue. It was going to be a thousand times worse with four mates to one hybrid, and that had never happened in our long history.

Xenon went out and shut the door behind him. I was left alone with Sybil. She brought me a glass of water and warned me to drink it slowly. It wasn't blood, but it helped. While I was relieving my parched throat, Sybil looked at me curiously.

"The entire Order is looking into this mate situation. It's not part of the hex as you think. We removed all traces of the hex. You've been out for two weeks. Your mates just woke up two to three days ago, and we realized what was happening. The theory right now is that since you are a hybrid, Nature gave you four potential mates and there's supposed to either be a spell to find out your true mate, or it's a gift from Nature, and you will get a choice in your mate."

My throat finally didn't feel like sandpaper. "We've

been working together for over five hundred years. I'm like their kid sister."

"I'll let them explain all that to you, but I don't think the situation is exactly like you think it is. They are coming in now and try to remember, Liliana, dragons, and Lycans are *very* possessive of their mates."

I already knew that and Quinn, and Jago burst in the room first. I half expected a shoving match, but they each rushed to a side of my bed and offered their necks. They knew I only fed from their wrists and I found myself *wanting* to bite their necks. Colnar and Cirrus both stood at the foot of my bed, and they all looked too worried about me to fight just yet. I still wasn't quite sure this wasn't part of the hex in the magic bomb.

"Please, love, you need blood. We talked before we came in and we won't fight over who you pick," Jago said. That was when it hit me. He called me love when we were trying to get here, and we were just in too much danger and pain for me to realize it. He *never* called me that before. Had this all started in the air?

I remembered what I'd been told, and I already knew that was a promise they couldn't keep. I had been trained as a diplomat first, and that was what I needed to be now.

"Please, I'm going to need a lot of blood to heal. More than one of you can give right now. I'll bite all of you from youngest to oldest."

Quinn was practically gloating. He was much older than me, but the youngest of the group. Xenon told them to behave while I was healing, but he scooped me up and pressed me to his hard chest. Quinn was huge, almost seven-feet-tall, like most Lycans, with chestnut hair that brushed his shoulders and bright blue eyes. He also smelled amazing now that I was in his arms.

He smelled like musk and mahogany. Now that I had my face pressed into his neck, I couldn't help giving him a few love nips. My long, black hair was hiding my face, and the others wouldn't see and get jealous. Quinn just had to give me away. He growled and pulled me closer to him.

I gave his neck one last lick of my tongue and sunk my fangs in. I'd had Quinn's blood before, but never like this. Never from the neck and never after Nature had marked us mates. Quinn's blood exploded in my mouth like a thousand little orgasms. I'd never had blood do this to me. If I hadn't been starving and recovering, I would have demanded he take me on the bed right then and there, damn the consequences.

I barely managed to pull myself away from him before I took it too far and landed him back in bed. I pulled away practically shaking. I was right. The pull to my mates I had been feeling the entire time I was out was exactly what I needed.

Colnar cleared his throat. "Step aside, Lycan. It's my turn."

I had enough strength to wrap my arms around Colnar's neck and bury my face in his neck. Colnar was all Incubus. Long black hair and inky black eyes. He smelled like incense and sex. I'd only felt his sexual energy once, and that was when I knew the mate-pull started when we were in the air. We were all hurting, but Colnar *wanted* me to feel it then because he could certainly aim it now.

I groaned as I watched the swirling purple sexual energy coming off Colnar dive directly into my stomach.

I felt a warm, tingly feeling all the way to my toes and was a little rough when I bit him. His fingers clutched my back.

His lips leaned forward to brush my ear. "You'll find I like it a little rough, beloved," he whispered. "You can bite me like that whenever you want."

I groaned and withdrew my fangs. I didn't want to let go of Colnar or his sexual energy, but if I didn't, I'd have an angry Fae and a pissed off dragon and to be honest, I wanted to taste both of them too.

The Fae mostly thought vampires were dirty for blood feeding, but Cirrus happily hopped in my bed when Colnar moved away. "Make it sting a little, pet," he said, pulling me to his chest. Quinn growled and Jago sort of let out this snort because he said that loud enough for everyone to hear.

If Colnar was dark and sexy, Cirrus was beautiful in a totally different way. I tangled my hands in his long red hair and gave it a little pull as I nipped at his neck. Cirrus had this look of beautiful innocence about him like all the light Fae did. It gave them an edge in battle because they were deadly warriors. I was a little surprised he was all for me biting him and wanting it to hurt.

I pricked his neck several times with my fangs, lapping at his blood before I bit him for real. He pulled my hair right back and let out this huge groan loud enough for the entire room to hear. Jago huffed again. He was the oldest and had to wait his turn. I think he would have preferred a quick feed, then me taking my time with him, but I'd never had this much fun feeding before. I'd bitten human lovers during sex and compelled them to forget, but it was nothing like this.

Cirrus was shaking when I stopped feeding, and I'd

wondered if I took too much. He was dazed when I let go and held him at arms distance. "I've always been told Fae don't let vampire's feed off them because something about the bite reacts with Fae blood. I thought it was something bad, but it's kind of like drinking too much expensive Fae wine."

"Get your drunk, Fae ass in a chair and settle down. It's my turn now," Jago growled.

Jago was the oldest and bigger than any Lycan I'd ever met. He was one of the last of his kind, and I had no idea how it was supposed to work if he wasn't mated with another dragon. Jago had skin the color of the darkest night and amber eyes that seemed to have a ring of green around them. I'd always found Jago beautiful, I just never thought we'd end up here.

Jago was gentle when he took me in his arms. I expected him to be rough given his size and being a dragon. I realized my mistake when his lips brushed my ears. "You've always been my treasure, and now you're my mate. I never thought this possible, but I'm glad it happened, my treasure."

I was so confused. Had Jago been secretly in love with me this entire time? The vein in his neck pulsed and his blood called to me. I'd find that out later. I think we all needed to have a conversation about why they all seemed so accepting of this.

Jago was so gentle with me since he considered me his treasure. I let my lips gently caress his neck, and I tried to make the bite sting less. Like the other three, I practically heard music and saw stars with his blood. Now that I'd had all their blood after Nature made us mates, I wasn't thinking about hexes anymore. Something about this just felt right. A hex couldn't do that.

It should have taken me several more days to recover, but my body was practically singing, and I wanted out of this bed. All four of these men were calling to me, and I wanted to spend more time with them.

Xenon already knew where this was headed, and I knew what he wanted. He wanted to keep us apart until The Order had an answer. Now that I knew and had their blood, I didn't think I *could* be away from them. I'd had this crush on Xenon for years knowing full well he thought of me as one of his daughters. He always had trouble telling me no.

He just sighed. "You can't show your face in Russia again. Zimin will do what all dictators do and try to expand. Take your pick. Go to one of your villas around Russia and be with your mates if you're intent on figuring this out on your own. Stay close to a territory Zimin may take, and you already have control over. I'll try to keep orders to a minimum while you figure this mess out."

Xenon thought it was a mess and deep down, I knew it was. It really could have been a hex from that magic bomb if something like that was actually possible. Now that I was thinking straight, I knew it wasn't. I had thought we had all been hexed to *think* we were mates, but now that I'd had their blood, I knew it was Nature. Blood didn't lie, and a hex couldn't have changed their blood in a way that fooled me.

Xenon seemed to think this was a huge disaster, but it just felt right. I wasn't thinking about picking someone or what the fallout would be. I wasn't thinking about what would happen to the others if I did pick just one. I was full of the best blood I had ever had, and I was way too satisfied to be thinking of what would happen later.

PRESENT DAY

I still remembered that day, five years ago, when I seriously thought having four mates wasn't going to end badly when Aria called. After three years of trying to pick and get to know them, I wanted all of them, and none of the spells I'd come up with had given me the answer.

My four ancient warriors had been reduced to sixteen-year-old human boys. Fists fights were a daily occurrence; the taunts became more and more juvenile. It was unattractive, and I couldn't be alone with any of them without all of them freaking out. After my last attempt with a goblet failed, I did what I knew I had to do, but was dreading.

I couldn't pick. There was no way in Tartarus. I was hoping my goblet would take that burden away from me. There was this huge, screaming argument when I told them just to leave. They felt rightly betrayed by me that I couldn't pick. Instead of being mad at each other, they were mad at me. That was what I wanted though. Them not fighting, even if it meant they were furious with me.

I promised to work on figuring this mess out. Xenon was also mad at me for not having guards, but I just wanted to be alone.

I was shocked when Xenon portalled to the villa I was hiding in to tell me Aria Emanuele found herself in the same situation I had gotten myself in. She was kind of blindsided. Her mother had the Infinity Coven looking into her mates and just sort of sent them to her intending to tell her over the phone.

When I found out she'd be in Turkey where I was hiding out, I had the Red Sky pack give her my failed goblet and my phone number. One of her mates was the Infinity Coven heir, and if anyone could figure it out, it was going to be him.

I was hoping she'd call first, but I knew she wouldn't with everything going on. I called her after pacing my villa hoping she'd had an answer for me. I also needed to give her the next orders she would have for the Universal Army. She had no idea The Order founded it, but she was one of our best spies.

We caught Cade, and I heard about the punishment dealt to Unseen Moon. I didn't go there myself because I just couldn't. Hybrids had always been told to stay away from other hybrids because it would make supes nervous and they would try to hurt us. I wanted to be there helping to find out the answer for this mate mess, and I knew Aria's father would keep me safe, but I didn't want to put everyone in danger.

I was starting to think she came up with the same solution I had. It had been four days since the judgment against Cade. Maybe there wasn't an answer, and this was truly a curse. My phone finally rang, and it was her. She didn't give me the chance to talk.

"Liliana? I'm about to give you the best news of your life!" Aria said.

"You figured it out?"

"Rainer did. It's—Kalon, stop!"

Was Kalon her mate? Did it have to be someone from your nature? I didn't have a vampire or warlock mated to me. I hoped she wasn't about to tell me none of my mates belonged to me, but then I heard Ronric growl, and it wasn't like he was trying to kill someone this time. It was a playful growl.

"I plan on doing that to you too, princess," Ronric said.

Ronric and Kalon were both there and not trying to kill each other?

"They are *all* your mates, Liliana. You don't have to pick one, and there's a way to fix it so that they aren't all trying to kill each other. If you tell us where you're staying, Rainer can get you the exact spell and help you channel."

"But how—"

Aria just laughed. "Don't ask me. Nature confirmed it, and it's quite nice having the four of us together now that they are all getting along. Rainer! Magic fingers away while I'm on the phone!"

She sounded like she was deeply in love and having a blast. Could I have that? I just realized what she said. "You know what they say about us being together."

"Oh, it's time for that stupid rule to be broken. No one is going to be dumb enough to come against my mates and me and you and yours once they are all together. Besides, I have a feeling you need me right now."

She hardly knew me, but she was right. I needed

something or someone right now. I was alone in my villa, and I was lonely. I wanted my mates, but I would take the company. I'd have to find them now. They were scattered across the globe fighting to forget me. They wouldn't have run from a fight. They wouldn't have run from World War III. But they needed to get as far away from me as possible after what I did to them, and I understood that.

I reached out telepathically to Rainer and gave him the location. I was going to need all the support I could get. Maybe if my mates saw Aria with hers, they'd understand this could work.

If they would actually answer when I called.

5 YEARS AGO

I portalled all of us to my villa in Turkey. The wards were old, so I asked everyone to go inside while I refreshed them. It must have been something new with the mate-pull because instead of going inside to their usual rooms, they stood off to the side and were practically drooling as I waved my hands and chanted.

"You've always been sexy when you cast, pet," Cirrus said, licking his bottom lip.

"Always?" I asked leading them inside. I thought this was as new for me as it was for them.

Xenon knew we were coming here and someone had already prepared a meal. "Sit, and we'll explain, beloved," Colnar said.

We all prepared food and I sat and stared at them. They all had pet names for me, and they hadn't fought yet. They seemed just to accept this while I was wondering why. I always wondered what it would be like to date one of them instead of being hung up on Xenon all the time, but I didn't want to mess up our working relationship, and I didn't think they thought of me that way.

"You really haven't noticed, Liliana?" Colnar asked. I just blinked. Noticed what? He tipped his beer at me. "We've all been in love with you for centuries. We talked about it. You stuck us all in the friend zone for some reason, so we never pushed it. How do *you* feel about all this? You weren't that into us before."

"But...you all dated and fed. I thought about it, but I didn't want to ruin things and...and—"

"And you were in love with Xenon," Quinn finished softly. "You smelled differently around him. I always knew. You really didn't notice us stop flirting and Colnar putting off his feeds?"

I didn't. Did I really have my head up my ass so much I never noticed? "Have you been feeling what I'm feeling this entire time?"

"No," Jago said. "After a few years guarding you, we were all in love with you, but we never made a move because we were waiting for you to get over Xenon. I guess it took Nature for that to happen."

"How is this going to work? I still don't understand why Nature gave me four mates. Am I supposed to be with one of you or all of you?"

Quinn started growling, and steam started coming from Jago's nostrils. That was when I knew it could only be one. I knew full well how possessive dragons and wolves were. I just nodded that I understood, but I still didn't know how this was supposed to work.

"I've an idea," Jago said. "You give us each a week to romance you alone. The others will get a hotel. After that, we will all meet together, and Liliana can choose. This time, we go oldest to youngest."

Everyone grumbled, but they packed a bag and left. I was alone with Jago. I couldn't help but go to him and stroke his cheek. My skin was the color of coffee, but Jago's was much darker. I loved the contrast of our skin. He felt cool under my hand and he nuzzled my hand.

"My treasure," he sighed. He picked me up like I weighed nothing and carried me over to the sofa. He sat down with me in his lap and started rubbing his face in my neck. I shivered.

"How is this supposed to work, Jago? I'm not a dragon, and I can't have an egg as a dragon mate would."

He ran his fingers through my hair. "Easy. Our child would be stronger and wouldn't need it. You're stalling, my treasure. Are you nervous?"

"A little," I said, clutching his muscular arm and arching my back as he kissed my neck. "I've only been with humans. Won't we mark ourselves as mates?" I was practically writhing in his lap. I could feel his erection through my pants, and it was bigger than anything I'd been with before.

"Ah, only if we want to. I have to acknowledge you to Nature that I accept you as my mate first. It's kind of like Quinn if he decides to claim you before we've figured out what this all means. Do you really just want to talk now that I have you to myself?" Jago asked, nipping at my ear. "Your body is saying you don't want just to chat."

"Just answer me one thing," I said, pulling away from his hot mouth on my ear. "Do you and Quinn get a choice? If you don't acknowledge me and he doesn't claim me, can you both just walk away?"

I was still pressed against Jago's hard chest, and I felt it rumble as he chuckled. "It doesn't work like that. We're both going to be fighting the urge to do it and mark you before we've figured out what's going on. My dragon knows you're its treasure and mate now. He wants to acknowledge you to Nature and the world. And both of us like this little wriggling thing you're doing in my lap," he grunted, digging his fingers into my back.

Jago's eyes were green and gold with a slit down the middle. I had time to find out what all the ceremonies meant. I was sitting in the lap of a beautiful dragon, and right now, he was mine. I readjusted myself so that I was straddling his lap.

"Oh, you like this?" I asked, grinding myself harder into his erection.

I felt Jago's hot breath as he attacked my neck. "Little hybrid, didn't your mother teach you not to poke dragons?"

I'd never talked like this to anyone before. Something about Jago was making me bold. I ground into him harder and nipped at his neck. "Ah, Jago, it feels more like you've got something poking *me*."

I felt the steam blow from Jago's mouth. He picked me up and carried me to my bedroom. I knew I was supposed to be spending this time getting to know all of them on the romantic side so I could pick, but right then, all I wanted was to be naked with Jago.

Jago was panting and looking like he wanted to ravish me, but he set me on the bed gingerly. "My treasure," he said with an almost reverence, stroking my cheek. Jago gently kissed the corner of my mouth. "It's so hard not to take you out outside in the garden and acknowledge you."

Damned if I didn't want him to. I had no idea what it entailed or what would happen if he did. I didn't have the gift of foresight, but something just felt right about it. If it involved making love in the moonlight, I'd never done that before, and now I desperately wanted to.

"I can tell you're thinking about it, treasure. Once I do it, I can't take it back. My dragon wants you in the garden naked so I can speak the words, then he can mark you. None of us know what it will do if that happens. If we can all mark you as mates, I *will* kill the others for touching my treasure."

"Do you want to wait? Why did you bring me to my bed with things so complicated?"

Jago chuckled and started nibbling on my collarbone. "Dragons aren't like Lycan. My dragon isn't going to poke through and go out of control trying to mark you while I'm with you. I'm a shifter like Quinn, but we are totally different. I can show you *exactly* how much I've been pining for you to get over Xenon and look my way."

"I'm sorry—"

"Ah, Liliana," Jago sighed, coming up to kiss the corner of my mouth again. "First love takes the longest to leave you. You will never forget. I still remember mine. But here I am with you. I've loved you in secret for hundreds of years, and now Nature has made it possible for me to show you. May I show you, treasure?"

He'd kissed my neck and the corner of my mouth, but now I was aching for a deep kiss from him. "Kiss me, Jago," I pleaded.

He cradled my face in his palms and stroked my cheeks with his thumbs. "You will only need ask, never beg."

Jago brought his lips down softly to mine. A feathery soft kiss that set my body on fire. I arched my back and caressed his bottom lip with my tongue. I tangled my fingers in his dreadlocks and pulled him closer to me. He hesitated, pulling away briefly.

"You can bite me all you want," he purred, giving me permission.

His kisses were more insistent this time, his tongue caressing mine. I pricked his tongue with my fang and started sucking on his tongue. Jago groaned and started rubbing his erection into my stomach. My body was on fire as his hand crept up my shirt. My bra hooked at the front, and his deft fingers had it unhooked in seconds.

I started tugging on his shirt. I wanted to feel his naked chest on mine. I wanted to be totally naked with him, but he seemed to want to take his time. He lazily stripped his shirt off, and I traced the tattoos on his chest. He slowly unbuttoned my shirt and peeled it back. He said he could control his dragon, but his eyes were practically glowing.

"*My* treasure," he growled, his eyes roaming over my body.

"Touch me, Jago."

"How does my treasure wish to be touched?"

I squirmed. I didn't know or care how I just wanted his hands on me. He said he didn't want me to beg, but I think he wanted to hear it a little. Maybe not. He didn't give me a chance to speak. He brought his mouth down and bit my nipple. When they said dragons were fond of their treasure, they weren't joking.

I was panting and moaning, and Jago hadn't even gotten my trousers off yet. I was a mess when he finally got to my zipper and started tugging my trousers down my legs. He tossed them aside and started kissing my ankles.

"Are you going to leave those on?" I asked, eyeing his

jeans. I'd never tried this before because I'd only slept with humans and I didn't want to tip them off, but my best friend growing up was a little more adventurous than I was and told me about a little trick we could do with our magical light. I had a beautiful dragon, and I wanted to experiment with.

I sat up and focused my magic to my fingertip. I sent it all to Jago as I trailed my finger down his chest to his zipper. "Have you ever been with a witch before?"

Clearly, Fawn didn't lie to me. Jago's eyes were closed in contentment, and his chest was heaving. "You're the first witch and vampire. Is that a witch trick or a hybrid trick?" he asked as I tugged his jeans off.

"You can thank my friend Fawn for that. You're the first I've tried it on. I wasn't sure if she was feeding me a line of bullshit."

Jago practically tackled me. "No bullshit. I'd like to see what that can do while you're biting me, but I'm not done with my treasure yet. I intend to have her screaming my name and pulling my hair, and I haven't even gotten started yet."

Jago kissed his way down to my thighs. I sighed and willingly parted them. He licked and nipped my inner thighs for what seemed like ages like he had done my breasts. I was back to squirming and panting. I thought he was about to lick by my knee again, but he suddenly went between my legs and gave me a long lick. I clutched my silk sheets and arched my back.

Jago's tongue was rough, and I could tell it was forked. His dragon was poking out. Jago said he could control him, so I just lost myself to pleasure as his tongue flickered over my clit. I moaned his name when he worked his fingers inside me. I was wondering if I would have felt something like this before if I had taken another supe as a lover before or if Jago was just that damned good.

That dragon tongue was definitely a perk because he could flick it faster than any human or non-dragon could. I could feel the biggest orgasm I'd ever had before building, and I just surrendered to it when it hit me. I bucked on the bed, pulling Jago's dreadlocks and screaming his name.

He looked up from between my legs when I'd finally settled down. His forked tongue flickered at me, then went back to normal. He grinned at me.

"I don't have little witchy fingers, but there are advantages to being a dragon. That was only the beginning."

I touched his shoulder and sent a little magic through my fingers. He closed his eyes, and a little rumbling sound came from his chest. I'd never heard anything like that before. "My dragon likes your witchy fingers."

"I can hear that. Does he want to see what else they can do?" *I* wanted to see what else it could do. I wanted to use my magic to see how loud his dragon would make that little rumbling noise again.

Jago chuckled. "I said I could control my dragon, but he's never met you and those witchy fingers before. If you break them out again, I may throw you over my shoulder, carry you to the garden, acknowledge you and mark you in one go."

"So, what do we do instead?"

"The next best thing. You've never had a dragon before, I've never had a hybrid. May I make love to you?"

"Please. I'd love for my first supe to be your dragon."

Jago's dragon made that rumbling noise again. I took it to mean it was his happy noise. Jago positioned himself between my legs, and I felt him rub his cock along my slit. I had no idea if it was because he was a supe or a dragon, but it was bigger than any human I'd been with. I had no idea dragons could purr like cats, but that rumble became a constant thing as Jago was pressing into me.

If I could have purred myself, I would have as I took all of Jago. I wrapped my legs around his waist as his cock was buried deep inside me. He started slow, and this had never happened to me before, but I found I was unable to stop myself from clutching his buttocks and sending my magic through him.

"Little hybrid, my dragon is wanting to make sure *no one* else touches this treasure," he growled, speeding up. The rumbling in his chest was getting louder, and I knew I should stop, but I sent another jolt of magic through Jago. I *wanted* him to make sure no one else touched me. It just seemed right.

Jago thrusted into me harder. I dug my nails into his taut ass and screamed his name as I came again. Jago's dragon was rumbling so loudly the mirror on my wall was shaking, and he was working my pussy at a relentless pace. I could feel myself about to come again. Jago's dragon rumble became a roar as we both came together.

Jago nuzzled my neck as his roar became a purr again. "You're the most precious treasure ever, Liliana. It's going to be hard for me to leave when it's not my turn with you."

I'd been so wrapped up with Jago, and I hadn't even thought about my other mates or what was going to happen in the future.

PRESENT DAY

A ria apparently didn't waste time. I was expecting her in a few days, but a portal opened in my living room, not twenty minutes after we spoke — just enough time for them to pack. Aria looked like she wasn't used to portal travel, the same as she did when she arrived at the farmhouse to pick up Cade. I wondered if she hated it so much, Rainer just didn't do it. It was so much faster than a car. The day the magic bomb went off and sealed my mates if I hadn't been injured, I could have opened one and got us all out of there so much faster.

"I so prefer my Harley," Aria groaned, looking a little green.

"It gets easier the more you do it," I said with a small smile. Growing up, Aria had been my idol as the first hybrid and all the stories surrounding her. Sometimes, I thought I never measured up to her. It was nice to see she wasn't totally perfect.

Aria still looked a little disoriented, and I'd only met

her once, briefly, but she walked over to me and gave me this huge hug like we were old friends.

"Have you reached out to them yet? Part of the reason I wanted to come is that if they can see my mates and me together, they'll understand why they need to drink from the cup and drink blood like a vampire."

She hadn't explained all of the details about how her mates weren't all trying to kill each other right now, but apparently, I was on the right track with my goblet. I already knew none of my mates were going to drink blood. Cirrus would think it was beneath a Fae and Quinn and Jago would probably think it was going to do something bad to their beasts.

Aria could already see what I was thinking, but it was Ronric that spoke. "I'll talk to your shifter mates and let them know it's done nothing to my wolf. I'm not even going to try to talk sense into a fairy."

"The Infinity Coven has good relations with the Fae. I can talk to him," Rainer promised.

"Liliana and I need girl time," Aria said.

All of my villas had a rec room for me and my body-guards. I enjoyed a good beer and round of darts or pool too, and we played together frequently until Nature sealed us as mates. I gave them directions and asked Aria if she wanted something to drink. I had no idea where her preference lay, but I had a fully stocked bar because between the five of us that normally lived here, we had varied tastes.

"Do you have a bottle of good red wine? If I drink any more whiskey, I'm going to sprout chest hair. It's the favorite of all my mates. It was probably the one thing they could agree on for a while."

"Did you have a bunch of centuries-old children on

your hands?" I asked, handing her a goblet of wine. "I thought I was supposed to be the supernatural infant among us."

"Not children. More like horny college students. I guess they thought since I'm half Succubus if they all walked around with hardly any clothes on, I'd get horny and magically pick them, but my Succubus side doesn't work like that."

I started laughing. I'd already heard about how part of Cade's downfall was that he recognized Kalon from a photo of him in a thong. "So, you had naked men all over the house? I would have preferred that to what mine did."

"Naked men having a pissing contest. Part of the reason I never played with more than one man before them was that I loathe men fighting over me. I was about to punch both Ronric and Rainer in the face and kick them out the flat to sort themselves when I felt Kalon was in trouble."

"You know, I actually thought I would like having men fight over me. Isn't that supposed to be some women's fantasy? I hated every minute of it. Mainly, because I hated seeing the strong men I'd been working with reduced to insults and taunts."

"I think that fantasy only works in movies or porn where the woman picks and everyone is somehow okay with it, or it's got its own category on a porn channel."

I found myself blushing. I wasn't that familiar with human porn, and I stayed away from supe porn on encrypted channels. I'd probably done some of the things on those channels with my mates, but I didn't watch it.

"Um, Liliana?" Aria said, clearing her throat. "I can see you're embarrassed, but you're going to have to get over any hang-ups about sex pretty quickly when they come back, and it comes to marking you. Rainer and Kalon marked me *together*. Your mates might want to do that with you, and it just might have to go down that way since you were all made mates at the same time."

"At the same time?" I gulped. I could hardly handle one of them at a time, and there was no way they would go for that.

"Trust me. Once you've done it once, it's going to be what you want to do all the time. And once everyone is blood bound, they will be all for it."

I slouched in my seat. "Aria, I don't think they are going to come back to hear me out. They weren't just hurt I sent them away, they were angry with me for not being able to pick. They aren't going to forget that and come running back when I tell them the solution is sharing. I don't even know if they kept the same phone numbers."

Aria wrinkled her nose. "Please, don't use a cell phone. They are so impersonal when we can talk telepathically. The reason I got blindsided with my mates was that my mother was trying to call me on my phone in the middle of World War III when I was trying to work a mark."

I was surprised she was against technology given our line of work. Especially since she just joined the Order. We had top of the line tech. Some of the tech humans had their hands on was developed by shell corporations by supes in the Order. Now, it was my turn to preach to her. She'd given me a lecture on sex, and now I was giving one to her about what was expected in the Order.

She just rolled her eyes. "Sorry, I know I'm going to have to get used to that and sniper rifles, but you'll never convince me a cell phone is more secure than telepathy. And if you're contacting your mates to convince them to come back, if you actually want them to listen to you, if you do it telepathically, they don't have the option to decline the call."

"No, but they can put up a block as soon as they hear my voice."

"Liliana, they are probably just as miserable as you are and hoping to hear from you. Come on, sweetie, you deal with politicians. Dealing with angry mates will be a distant memory once they are all here and they've marked you."

That was easy for her to say. Aria didn't see the looks on their faces when I sent them away.

5 YEARS AGO

I should have foreseen how this mate situation was going to end up when my week was up with Jago and Cirrus showed back up. The others stayed away like they promised and I found myself missing them. I was glad to see Cirrus when he showed up, even though I would miss Jago, but Jago certainly didn't want him there.

As soon as Jago saw Cirrus, his dragonhide came out, and his eyes went to slits. Cirrus dressed carefully for this meeting. Tan linen trousers and a flowing white shirt that was open at the chest. It set off his red hair, which he had tied back at the front to show off his ears instead of hiding them like usual.

Jago's dragon started rumbling, and he pulled me to his chest. Cirrus just rolled his eyes like he expected this from all shifters and didn't comment when Jago gave me a possessive kiss before stalking out in a huff. Cirrus was practically tapping his toe waiting for him to leave. He gave me an easy smile once we were alone. I wondered if he was going to take me straight to bed and that was where we were going to spend our entire week like with Jago.

"Can I cook for you, Liliana? Proper Fae food?" That was when I noticed he had a bag with him.

"If you'll let me sit with you while you cook and teach me the recipe. The few times I've had Fae food, I've loved it."

"Deal," Cirrus said.

He knew his way around the kitchen. We had servants here, but they didn't do everything. We all took our turns cooking for everyone. Cirrus couldn't get ingredients to cook Fae food here. Fae could make portals like witches could, so he must have gone back home just to cook or maybe talk to someone about our situation.

"What are you cooking?"

"All my favorites. Roasted Cloud Finch, Jasmine Cookies, Sautéed jackrabbit, and Stone Nut Souffle."

"Jasmine cookies? I love those! A Fae ambassador brought some as gifts when I was just a child. I remember making myself sick sneaking off and eating all of them while my parents were discussing business."

"It's not Fae to admit this or do this, but I've done the exact same thing when Jasmine Cookies were involved."

I laughed. "Aren't you Fae royalty? You couldn't do what you wanted?"

"If you're my brother. You really think I'd be off galivanting with the Order if I were next in line? I was my parent's tenth child and let's just say they don't miss me."

"I miss you when you aren't here. Even before this mate stuff started, I always missed you when you were away on Fae business."

"Did you know the Fae can tell a lie from the truth? It

means a lot to me that you did miss me before. The Fae are against mixing, but I've never liked that rule. You intrigued me from the moment I saw you training. You have this delicate beauty about you, but you were so strong, even then."

I laughed. "I didn't think so. I agreed to join, but I had no idea what they were thinking of asking me. I was sure I was going to let everyone down."

"I knew you wouldn't just watching to try to learn the staff. You never gave up until you had a move mastered, even if you were hurt."

"You're sweet, Cirrus."

"Don't tell anyone that, okay? I've got my spoiled, Fae prince reputation to protect."

"I never thought of you that way, Cirrus."

"I know. That's part of why you caught my fancy. You just saw me as Cirrus. This is a huge mess, but I've gotten to know you, Liliana, and I know you'll figure this out in a way that works for all of us, even those possessive shifters."

"Fae don't even get a little bit possessive?" I asked. I wanted Cirrus to admit a fault about the Fae because sometimes he did act a little superior.

Cirrus laughed. "I'm going to let you in on a little Fae secret. This can't leave this room. The Fae are famous for their orgies. Even mates go. Where do you think the Romans got it from? Everyone wears masks, and it's like big sex parties. Witches dance naked under the moon during certain moon phases. The Fae have their own way of celebrating lunar phases."

I felt this foreign emotion that was probably jealousy. "Cirrus, I don't want to hear about orgies you've attended or you being with other women."

Cirrus just shrugged. "To the Fae, gender doesn't matter at these parties. What I'm trying to tell you, Liliana is that if you can get the Lycan and the dragon over their natures, Colnar and I have shared before. Incubus parties are much raunchier than a Fae party, but they do happen."

"Can you really tell me you had no problem with Jago kissing me like that before he walked out?"

Cirrus set a plate of delicious looking food in front of me. "Jago reminded me of a dog marking a tree with that kiss. It bothers me that Jago thinks of you as *his* and when Quinn gets here, he will think the same. You're our mate, but not our property. That's what bothers me. You should be our equal, like you've always been."

"Are you going to feel like that after we have our week and then you have to leave me with Colnar?"

Cirrus laughed. "I will admit to not wanting to leave you with an Incubus. I have several Fae tricks I intend to show you, but I can't exactly do what Colnar can."

"Fae tricks?"

"I hear witches can do it too. Fae call it Illumination, and we're using a different kind of magic, but the effects are the same. I hope you have no idea what I'm talking about."

I laughed. "My best friend, Fawn, already explained that little secret to me, but I've never had it done to me before."

"Well, then thank your friend Fawn because I've never had it done to me either. Illumination is not just for sex, but when it is, it's only done between mates. I've never done it to anyone either."

"Then we'll share it together." He didn't ask me if I'd done it before and I was glad because my first time was with Jago. I didn't want Cirrus to know this because I didn't want to hurt him. "This food is amazing, Cirrus. Where did you learn to cook?"

"For a prince you mean? Fae royalty, like my brothers and sisters, they wouldn't know. My siblings probably have someone wipe their asses for them. I left to join the Fae army when I was eighteen. I came to the Order's attention during the territory wars. I learned to cook from other soldiers."

I cocked an eyebrow at him. "You made Jasmine cookies on the battlefield?"

"I learned those from a Fae lover in the Order. She was my first love and much older than me. I got clingy, and she got tired of me. That was that."

"So, you could get clingy over this mate situation."

"I like it when you tease me, you know. Enough to ruin this dinner I cooked by sweeping these plates off the table and taking you right here. If you keep that up, you won't even be able to try my Jasmine cookies."

I was thinking about his Illumination and Jago's reaction to my magic. "How about we save the Jasmine cookies and feed them to each other in bed?"

Cirrus' full mouth widened into a grin. "I like the way you think."

We ate the rest of the delicious meal at a pretty fast pace. I wasn't lying when I said Jasmine cookies were one of my favorites. Word got out I gorged on them, and every time a Fae ambassador came to my parent's court, they would give me a tin and a wink. I hadn't had them in so long because I'd been moving around manipulating governments. I think if Cirrus had known, he would have made them before now.

Cirrus grabbed the tray of cookies and took my hand,

practically dragging me back to my bedroom. He set the tray on the nightstand and started unbuttoning his shirt.

"Can I help it if now that you mentioned it, one of my fantasies is feeding you Jasmine cookies naked?"

I'd already started pulling my shirt off. Cirrus wasn't huge with muscle like Jago and Quinn. He had the body of a male dancer, and now that I was seeing him naked, he was beautiful. He hopped into my bed like he'd been there before.

"Come put your head in my lap."

I rested my head on his firm thighs, and he started stroking my hair. His Jasmine cookies were the best I'd had before. Buttery and soft with a hint of the Silver Jasmine that only the Fae knew how to cultivate.

"Oh, Cirrus, these cookies," I moaned.

"If I'd known they'd get you naked and, in my lap, I would have made them centuries ago."

"Maybe not on the first try, but definitely on the second."

He thankfully didn't mention my Xenon hang up. Xenon seemed like a distant memory. Cirrus was feeding me cookies with one hand and playing with my hair with the other. Like with Jago, I felt bold with Cirrus. I didn't give him any warning. I rolled over and took his cock in my mouth. I used the magic in my hands around his shaft.

Cirrus gasped and pulled my hair. I felt something pulsing in my hair, and it must have been his Illumination. He leaned forward and hauled my hips toward him. I felt his tongue on my clit, and I groaned on his cock. I finally realized what my fingers were sending out when his slipped inside me. I was quivering and shaking. Cirrus wasn't faring much better.

"Stop, please stop," he begged, pushing my shoulders away gently. "I'm going to explode everywhere if you keep doing that."

I was turned on and bold again. I crawled into his lap. I'd had him in my mouth, but I hadn't kissed him yet. I traced a trail of light down his chest and kissed him deeply. He cupped my ass and sent his Illumination through me.

"I don't think either of us is going to last long if we keep doing this," I groaned.

"You know what I've always fantasized about since I started having feelings for you?" Cirrus murmured, kissing my neck.

I ran my fingers through his hair and let them trace the point of his ear. "What would that be, Cirrus?"

"You, in my lap. Liliana, you're sexy as hell when you walk into a room of arrogant politicians and walk out with all of them your puppies. I know it's compulsion, but it enchanted me. I always imagined me just laying back and letting you do whatever you wanted to me."

I blinked. "That's so..."

"Not Fae. I know. There's just something so sexy about the idea of you on top of me."

"Well, I'm already here," I said. I started stroking his cock with just a little magic coming out my hands. Cirrus had a beautiful cock. It was long and thick, perfectly formed, and it was almost too thick for my hand. It curved upward at this arc, and I let my fingers trace it.

Cirrus wanted me in control. I'd never really explored that before, but I wanted to tonight. I wanted to torture Cirrus a little. I wasn't exactly gentle with the politicians I turned. Most of them were bad men, and I didn't feel bad at all that once I had them in a trance, I took as much blood as I wanted from them. A girl needed to feed.

I ran my thumb over the head of Cirrus's cock, sending a little more magic than before. He groaned. "Did I have this inside me in your fantasy?"

"Yes," he gulped. "When I pictured it, you were always shy at first, then you went wild and fucked me harder than anything I've had before."

I leaned forward and started tonguing the point of his ear while still stroking his cock. "Is that what you want, Cirrus? You have to tell me, or I won't do it."

Cirrus was shaking. "Maybe you didn't know how sensitive our ears are? Ride me, Liliana, then I want you to bite me right at the end."

I had no idea a Fae's ears were that sensitive. Cirrus was practically quivering. I gave the point of his ear one last lick. When I pulled back, Cirrus' hand was practically shaking when he caressed my cheek. His large green eyes were closed, and his long lashes framed them. I found myself liking having Cirrus practically begging. I wanted him to do it more.

I still kept up my fight training, even if I never used it. I sparred with Cirrus with the staff several days a week. My body was strong, even if the Order never required me to use it like a warrior. My thighs didn't complain at all when I hovered over Cirrus and just slid down far enough to take the head of his cock in me. I went right back to nibbling on his ears.

"Is this what you want?" I whispered in his ear.

I was expecting him to pull me all the way down on him and use his Illumination to punish me for teasing him. Jago would have. Jago probably would have flat out spanked me. I wasn't expecting Cirrus to be so submissive for a Fae and a Fae warrior at that. I rather liked this side of both of us.

"More, my witch," Cirrus pleaded, squirming. He really wasn't going to take anything. Cirrus had clearly been thinking about this. This was his fantasy, but I was in control and enjoying myself.

I slid down his cock a little more and started moving my hips in a circle. Cirrus hadn't used his Illumination again. If he had, this would be going much differently. I traced my tongue from his earlobe to the point of his ear. Cirrus grasped my ass and moaned. Who knew Fae ears were so much fun? Cirrus' reaction to me nibbling on his ears was turning me on even more. Just my tongue on his ear was like having his cock in my mouth again.

I wanted to draw this out even more, but the noises Cirrus was making, and the way he was clutching my ass had me desperate for all of him. I stopped my teasing circles and dropped down, taking all of Cirrus. I felt the pleasant burn of him stretching me. Cirrus gasped in surprise, and the Illumination he sent through my ass may have been involuntary, but it sent pleasant shocks through my body.

His eyes finally fluttered open. Cirrus had such pretty eyes. His eyelashes may have even been longer than mine.

"I want to watch you. Liliana, you have no idea how much I dreamed about doing this. I never thought it would happen."

I started slowly riding him, enjoying the feel of his cock and making his fantasy come true. "What do I do next in your dream?" I remembered Cirrus wanting my bite to hurt when I woke up. I didn't think I would be up for hurting him in bed if he was into that.

Cirrus finally used his Illumination again. "This is way

better than any dream I had about you. What do *you* want to do to me, Liliana?" he asked, sending another jolt through me.

I groaned and sped up. "Exactly what I'm doing right now, but I want to feel your hands all over me. You said you dreamed of me going out of control at the end. Make me feel like I want to go out of control, Cirrus, and I'll give you what you want."

Cirrus had been mostly submissive while I was sitting on his lap, but I saw the Fae warrior peek through when he cocked an eyebrow at me. I knew what that meant. Challenge accepted. As much as I wanted to make Cirrus' little fantasy come true, he was going to have to participate because I *never* lost control in anything I did. Sure, Jago brought things out of me I didn't know were there, but I'd worked damned hard to control my vampire side since I was a child. Cirrus and the rest of them knew this.

Cirrus finally sat up and started nipping my neck pretty hard. "If I turn your witch side on enough, will the vampire side come out to play?"

I laughed and ground into him harder. "Are you going to get goofy again?"

Cirrus growled and bit down on my neck right as he sent Illumination into my breast. I couldn't help speeding my hips up.

"Not goofy. I think they tell Fae not to let vampires bite them because after you bit me, I felt like I'd had good wine and a marathon sex session. If other Fae found out about it, they'd be lining up to get bit. They must tell us vampires are dirty bloodsuckers because it could get addicting."

Cirrus moved to my earlobe and kept a slow stream of

Illumination through his fingers as he rolled my nipple between his finger. Now *I* had a fantasy I wanted to act out too.

"So, if I bite you after a marathon sex session, you would feel good and, so would I?"

He moved his hand between us and started rubbing my clit with his thumb. I felt the slow hum of the Illumination coming from his finger — Yup, that was exactly what I needed for what Cirrus was wanting. He didn't have to say a word. I knew that was exactly what he wanted. He was still kissing my collarbone, and his neck was right there.

His Illumination and thick cock inside me were better than any vibrator I'd bought. I could feel my vampire blood starting to stir. It had woken up from the long sleep I'd put it in. Apparently, Cirrus could bring it out of hiding with that light from his fingers. I was starting to wonder which one of us was actually in control here.

I threw back my head and started wildly riding him. It was freeing to let my vampire side out like this. I wasn't angry or in danger of killing someone, which was the reason I kept it hidden. Cirrus had coaxed it out and was playing with it like he wasn't in danger from me.

Cirrus said he wanted me to do what I wanted to him, but he wasn't a passive participant anymore. He was just as wild as I was. He had one hand between us rubbing my clit and the other on my ass encouraging me to go faster and both hands were using his Illumination. He was biting my neck so hard he was getting close to breaking the skin, and I loved every minute of it.

Cirrus could tell I was close. He stopped his little bites and turned his head, so his neck was available to me. I sank my fangs into his neck right as my world exploded. Cirrus' blood hit my throat, and I bucked wildly on him. I had to force myself to withdraw my fangs before I hurt him — one of the dangers of letting my vampire side out to play.

I went to climb off Cirrus when I finally settled down, but he tightened his arms around me and pulled us both down to the bed. That drunk, goofy look he'd gotten from my bite when he was recovering was nothing compared to it now. For the life of me, I could never remember him getting like this when I bit him before. I had to ask.

Cirrus just laughed. "You didn't notice I was in a hurry when you interviewed me after you bit me? I had the erection from hell. Not even a cold shower fixed it."

"Did you go out vampire hunting for more bites after that?" I said, licking his ear again now that I knew his reaction.

"No, it was weird. I'd watched you train, and that was the first time I'd met you, but I knew even then you were the only one I wanted biting me. And if you keep doing that to my ear, you're not going to get any sleep tonight."

I didn't have my fangs out, but I bit his earlobe. I felt him get hard inside me and I grinned to myself. It was going to be a long night.

PRESENT DAY

I t had been three days since Aria, and her mates came to my villa. I'd still been putting off contacting my mates. No one was pushing me. Aria was half vampire too and knew just as well as I did since I'd had so much of their blood, I could easily locate them to contact them telepathically. If they blocked me, I would have their location to send a messenger from the Order. Xenon would probably portal there himself to order them to get their asses back to me.

I hadn't yet because I just wanted the company. I'd been alone for two years, ever since I sent them away. I'd spent time with the Red Sky pack, who were always entertaining and hospitable. I threw myself into finding the answer and helped end Zimin's reign. I couldn't show my face again because Zimin and his warlock had to think I was either dead or scared, but I was used to working in shadows.

I had just woken up, and it was very early. I'd been having trouble sleeping since I sent my mates away. I'd always slept alone before, but after sleeping with each of them, it was too hard now. And there was just this awful guilt that never went away that I couldn't pick. I knew now I wasn't supposed to, but the guilt was still there now because I should have figured that out before I hurt everyone.

I stopped when I got in the kitchen to turn the coffee maker on. Huge Ronric was sitting at the counter in just his boxers eating Quinn's sugary cereal like it was the best thing he'd ever eaten. Ronric seemed to love having his shirt off, but this was the first time I'd seen him without trousers too.

He just winked at me. "Love, don't tell Aria you found me in here going to town on children's cereal. I have a reputation to protect."

I flipped the coffee machine on and sat next to him. Ronric was a Lycan like Quinn. Maybe he could tell me exactly how badly I'd fucked up with Quinn.

"That's Quinn's cereal. Do all Lycans have a thing for kiddie cereal?"

He leaned over and bumped my shoulder with his. "Want to know a Lycan secret? We have a thing for cereal and junk food. You gain weight with it, and then you turn it into muscle. It's much more fun than those nasty human protein shakes and it's not like we have to worry about human diseases like diabetes. Quinn may have a thing for this cereal, but me, soda bread pudding from back home was my favorite to gorge on."

I found myself laughing for what felt like the first time in ages. "Quinn is from Wales. He doesn't just go for this cereal. It's a huge treat for all of us when he makes Eve's Pudding." My mood instantly soured, and I slumped in my seat. "They're all good cooks who have cooked a variety of food from their countries and clans.

I've royally fucked this up," I moaned, rubbing my eyes with my palms.

"It's not all on you, love. I've no idea what got into me once we were all together, but I acted like a hormonal pup instead of a fully grown Alpha. Tell me, did your Lycan and dragon claim you?"

"Jago kept saying he wanted to acknowledge me, but he could control his dragon. Quinn is only three hundred years older than I am. He started to a few times, but he stopped himself."

Ronric let out a deep-chested laugh. "Did Aria tell you I claimed her our first night alone together? I'd planned to do that from that start, no matter what it meant. I had no idea claiming her meant I was going to be able to feel when she was with the others, but I made a total ass of myself several times."

I shook my head. "I don't think that's a claiming thing, Ronric. My mates weren't exactly civil to each other either."

"No, you don't understand. I'm an Alpha. I don't need to one-up anyone. I never have before, and I knew deep down I didn't need to then. It's like I couldn't stop myself. Rainer and I knew we were pissing Aria off. I could smell it on her, but we kept doing it."

I finally smiled again, remembering some of the things Aria told me. "She said both of you walked around practically naked. Since you've marked her, why are you sitting in my kitchen in your boxers?"

He grinned, and I swore he flexed his biceps at me. "If it bothers you, I'll go put clothes on. I got hungry and didn't think anyone would be awake. Clothes are so restricting. If Aria finds out you saw me, she'll punch me in the gut again. She gets possessive like a wolf, but ever since her Ma saw me half naked, she gets mad at me for it now."

I cocked an eyebrow at him. "Why did Aria's mother see you with no clothes on?"

"The wench got tired of us holing up in Aria's bedroom fucking like bunnies instead of calling you. She broke in right when we were about to make another go at it, and I didn't pull enough covers over myself to Aria's liking."

"I'd probably hex you until you learned to behave."

Ronric threw back his head and laughed. "Yeah, you keep your Lycan mate in line. The dragon too. Shifters don't like clothes. They just get in the way."

"Can you give me advice as a Lycan? Did I totally blow things with Quinn?"

"Quinn is probably some sad puppy licking his wounds moping about just as much as you are right now. Your dragon is probably telling himself he's mad, but he's desperate to hear from you."

"Ronric, if you can imagine how you would have reacted if Aria made you all leave, that's about how it went down. They probably all hate me."

"I've already imagined that scenario as soon as Aria threw it out when she was pissed at us. I can already tell you what all of them are thinking. It's not anger at you. They are angry at themselves and thinking they aren't good enough for you. They think if they were worthy, you would have picked them. The dragon and your Fae may be deflecting and getting angry about it, but deep down, they all probably think you sent them away because they aren't really your mate and the real one is out there somewhere. When you meet them, you'll finally be able to choose. You're less likely to piss them off and more likely to give them peace if you call them."

I felt like something was pricking my skin. I didn't even have time to absorb what Ronric said it was so strong. I turned around, and Aria was in the doorway with her arms crossed glaring at Ronric. She didn't look mad at me; she looked furious with him, which surprised me.

"You just can't keep your trousers on, can you? Liliana has four mates she misses. You in your boxers isn't going to ease her pain, you big, stupid Lycan. What the hell are you eating?" she demanded, picking up the cereal box.

So, that's why she went after him and not me. I wasn't a threat to her because I had mates. I had a feeling if Ronric was eating cereal in his boxers with anyone else, they would be the one getting yelled at and glares instead of Ronric. He just grinned and pulled her into his lap like he loved her getting mad at him.

"Kaptain Kookie cereal. Quinn's favorite. He *has* to get this imported from America. They have the best sugar cereals there. You can help me turn it into muscle later. I was *helping* Liliana understand her mates. You forget I was in their situation almost."

Aria looked like she didn't know if she wanted to deck him or drag him back to their bedroom. I just kept talking about that ridiculous cereal Quinn liked so much.

"Quinn has a contact in The Order who is stationed in the States. She sends him care packages of American junk food all the time. I had no idea it was a Lycan thing to like junk. I thought it was one of Quinn's quirks."

Aria turned around and looked Ronric right in the eye. "Did you seriously just *lie* to Liliana and tell her Lycans are genetically disposed to eat children's cereal?"

Ronric just started laughing like she didn't look like she was about to go for his jugular. Maybe he was a little insane, but I didn't want blood in my kitchen. These countertops were expensive.

"I really don't think he's lying," I said, trying to save this mad Lycan from bleeding everywhere. "Quinn is nuts for this cereal too, and he's almost Ronric's size. Ronric explained Lycans can eat junk food to bulk up without getting sick."

Now, I was sure Ronric was crazy. "Jealous, princess?" he teased, nipping at her nose.

I was surprised when she didn't rip his throat out, she just turned around and leaned into his chest. "I wouldn't touch that cereal if you promised to do all my favorites. Did my big, stupid beast say anything to settle your mind?"

I sighed and just stared at the two of them. They made it look so easy. They had this easy banter that *should* have had her vampire side inflicting pain, but she seemed to love it when he gave her a hard time. I wondered if it would be like this if my mates forgave me and came back. Arguments settled with a simple nose nip and cuddling. I realized she expected an answer.

"Yes, a lot of what he said makes sense, but I just can't help remembering how bad it was the night I sent them away. We were all trying to figure things out longer than all of you were. I think they all hate each other now. Quinn would get into screaming arguments with Jago where the only words he could get out was just to scream *mine* over and over."

Ronric's brow furrowed. "Then Quinn claimed you. That was his wolf. I thought you said he didn't?"

Now, I was confused. This whole time, I thought

Quinn and Jago hadn't announced anything to Nature in case this went ass up. Neither of them did any type of ritual or said any words about sealing anything. Now, Ronric looked angry.

"Please tell me Quinn didn't claim you like a hormonal pup."

Aria and I both looked confused. I was guessing her claiming experience was much different than mine since I didn't even know it happened. Ronric rolled his eyes.

"Quinn might not have known he was doing it either," Ronric said, setting Aria off his lap.

The next thing I knew, he had his huge paws all over me pulling the neck back on my shirt. I slapped his hands away.

"Don't make me bite you or hex you. Quinn didn't mark me. I would have known and stopped him. You forget I'm different than Aria. I would have had to have marked him too."

"Get your hands off Liliana, or I'll bite you too," Aria threatened.

"Promise, princess?" Ronric grinned, yanking her back in his lap like she was a toy.

Before I knew it, Kalon and Rainer came stumbling into my kitchen. Thankfully, they both put trousers and a shirt on. They were all very attractive men, but I wasn't into them like that now that I had my mates. I think Aria knew that, but it probably would have put the mate drive in overload for her and someone would have gotten bitten.

"You are so loud, Ronric," Kalon moaned. "Why are you not in bed, *dragoste?*"

"Have you forgotten why we are here, Kalon?" Rainer asked. He was eyeing that Kaptain Kookie cereal with disdain. "Liliana, is it okay if I cook the adults in the room a civilized breakfast?"

I perked up. I was starving and I'd barely been eating since I sent everyone away. Sitting with Ronric in his boxers over children's cereal had settled my mind just a little bit, and my appetite had come back full force. I felt like I hadn't eaten food in years, which was mostly true. I'd been grazing instead of having full meals, and the only blood I drank was when Xenon showed up and made me. Rainer was from the Infinity Coven, and I loved Egyptian food.

"I think I have ingredients for *ful medames*," I said hopefully. That was my favorite breakfast and what I always started my morning with if I was visiting with Infinity.

Rainer gave me this gentle smile like he knew I was practically starving myself, both food and blood wise. I just didn't have an appetite. It was probably pretty obvious to anyone in the room too because my already slim body was even thinner.

"Your aura seems a little more at peace since we got here," he said as he dug through the fridge and pantry. "How about some Umm Ali to celebrate the small victories?"

I just nodded while my stomach growled. The energy around Aria was starting to pulse now that all her mates were here, but I shortly realized the reason.

"God, you're sexy when you cook," she purred. I was starting to wonder if I was going to get breakfast or they'd all disappear to the bedroom.

Ronric just nipped her ear and pulled her closer to his chest. "Focus, princess. Quinn might not have marked you, but he definitely claimed you. After I claimed Aria, we weren't mated yet, but I could feel her when her emotions were high. I didn't want to feel her having sex with these two assholes while I was trying to sniff out a warlock, but I could feel her when she got angry or upset. Do you understand what that means?"

"Yeah, Quinn claimed me after promising he wouldn't!" I don't know why I was so angry about that. We were going to have to do it anyway now, but he should have told me.

Ronric finally wasn't smirking or joking for once. "Quinn didn't claim you without telling you. Quinn's wolf took over and claimed you, and that was why you didn't hear something more poetic and were asked first. Quinn controlled his wolf after that and *didn't* mark you. Now that I've seen how all that works with all of us, if Quinn had claimed you and marked you, but you didn't mark him back, I think that's a sign to Nature you're rejecting him as your mate. I'm not sure what would have happened to Quinn after that. It's never been done before, but neither has any of this."

"He still should have told me after his wolf did it."

Ronric shrugged. "He might not have known. If you don't keep your wolf centered, it becomes an inner battle with him. If Quinn was injured as bad as the rest of you and didn't take the time to center because he wanted to be with you so badly, his wolf would be keeping secrets, and that was why you kept seeing him only able to yell *mine*. Quinn was fighting with his wolf."

I rubbed my face in my hands, and my newly found appetite was starting to slip away again. If Quinn still hadn't centered his wolf, he was probably enraged and would never come back.

"Liliana, every Lycan knows when things get to a

certain point, you center your wolf. Quinn probably just didn't want to leave you around the others to do it because he thought he'd lose you. Quinn is probably centered now and can feel what you're going through. If you contact him, he's probably been worried sick about you. He's probably a mess wanting to call you if he's just a pup."

"He's older than I am and I'm not an infant!" I snapped.

"You aren't a Lycan either. We age differently. He'll be considered a pup until he reaches the age of one thousand or so."

"Quinn is a grown man and a capable warrior! He's protected me in countless situations. Quinn was recruited into The Order a long time ago while you still think he's a baby," I reminded him.

Ronric just shrugged like I didn't understand Lycans. Maybe I didn't. I just watched a seven-foot-tall Lycan eat an entire box of sugary cereal meant for children.

"Let us change the subject," Kalon said. I shot him a grateful look. "Have your mates had your blood?"

"No, none of them are vampires. I'm still not quite sure how this is all going to work since I'm dual natured."

Rainer was fast. He started setting bowls of food and plates in front of us. I thought my appetite had gone away again, but as soon as I saw the boiled eggs arranged around the spiced fava beans, my stomach let out this huge growl.

"My cooking does that to people," Rainer grinned.

"Are you going to tell Liliana your big secret?" Aria flirted. "She's a witch too."

"You can add magical herbs like Devil's Garlic and Demon clove to the recipe that makes people enjoy it more. It's not hexing them. It just enhances the eating experience."

I just shrugged and dug into my food. I didn't care what was in it, it was delicious, and I hadn't sat down for a fully cooked meal in ages. I'd just judged Ronric for eating an entire box of cereal, but I ate three bowls of Rainer's food and still ate dessert.

I needed this. I needed the company. I'd been spending too much time alone wallowing. Ronric was rough around the edges, but between what he shared with me about his experience in their similar mess and how Quinn must be feeling, I thought I might be able to contact everyone now. Between Ronric and Rainer, the courage I normally had was slowly starting to come back.

I was finally starting to think I could be as happy as Aria and her mates.

Cirrus was certainly all Fae. He wanted what he wanted when he was in the mood for it. He spent his week with me portalling in and out to get Fae food and cooking for me, but in the bedroom, he was all over the place. He wasn't submissive, he wasn't dominant, he was just Cirrus and what he was in the mood for that night. And I loved every minute of it.

I knew I was going to miss him when he left, but I was actually petrified and looking forward to my week with Colnar at the same time. Now that I had experienced Fae Illumination and I'd had a taste of Colnar's sexual energy, I had no idea what was going to happen to me if he used it on me for a straight week.

When Colnar finally showed up, he let himself in and just leaned against the doorframe, his black eyes glaring at Cirrus. Cirrus said he hated what Jago did when he left me, and he didn't do the same, but he pulled me into a long hug.

"You can compel him not to turn you into his slave,"

he whispered in my ear. "It's the only thing I know to fight him off if he fights dirty to get you to pick him."

I didn't comment. I was nervous, petrified, about being with an Incubus, but I already knew Colnar wouldn't do that. Colnar kept late nights because of his nature and so did I because of work. Colnar and I talked when he came home from feeding if I was still awake. Colnar never took anyone to bed that wasn't out prowling for sex, and he actually hated feeding on so many anonymous men and women. Colnar had wanted to find his mate for a long time. Now that we both knew it was me, he wouldn't trance me to get me to pick him because I'd eventually figure out how to fight it and never speak to him again after hexing him impotent.

Cirrus kept looking over his shoulder on the way out and seemed to take forever to leave, but eventually, it was just Colnar and me. That confident, handsome, angular face was actually looking as nervous as I felt and he hadn't moved from the doorframe.

"What's wrong, Colnar?"

"It's just...you. This whole time we've been guarding you, you've only ever dated humans. I know you've been with a supe now that you've been alone with Jago and Cirrus. Your aura is different and the sexual energy coming off you is different than I'm used to. You've been with a dragon and a Fae now, and I know they each had their own abilities to pleasure you. You've never been with an Incubus before, and I don't know how to work this without you getting addicted to what I put out and take away."

"Are you hungry?" I asked. Colnar loved my cooking the most and had a thing for the Syrian and Turkish recipes I grew up eating. Colnar seemed very nervous for an Incubus and seemed to let out the breath he was holding when I suggested eating instead of anything else.

"Can you make your mother's Fatti recipe again?"

I just laughed and nodded. That was Colnar's favorite. I knew all of their favorite foods, even before Nature made us mates. I led him to the kitchen and set a tin in front of him.

"My father sent Lokum because he's trying to tempt me home for a visit," I said, turning to set ingredients on the counter.

"Do your parents know about us? I got the feeling they liked us as your bodyguards when we visited, but they won't like us as your mates. Your father would probably hex our cocks off, and I've always been afraid of your mother. She'd probably just bite it off."

I just laughed again because I wouldn't put that past her. My mother had mostly retired from fighting, but I knew she missed a good scrap. She'd never held it against me I didn't take after her with the sword. I think she didn't want that life for me, but she seemed to love it. And Colnar was right. That was exactly why I hadn't told them. It was hard hiding The Order from them, but so far, I'd managed.

"My parents aren't going to flip their shit because I met my mate. They'll be happy for me. But if they find out now, my mother will probably make you all fight it out gladiator style to the death, and I can't watch that."

"I'd win," Colnar scoffed. There was my arrogant Incubus. Colnar was sexy as hell, and he damned well knew it. I didn't think it was a coincidence his weapon of choice was a spiked whip.

"My mother wouldn't let you use weapons. It would be a battle of wits and fists for me," I pointed out.

Colnar just gave me this smirk. "Your little Fae thinks we are dirty for feeding on sex, and your Lycan and dragon think they have the upper hand because they can shift. If they are attracted to men in the slightest, I can have all of them out in seconds."

"Is that how you got Quinn to put his wolf away when we were riding on Jago? I don't get that vibe from Quinn at all."

"Your fairy was digging it too. I couldn't get a read on Jago because he had shifted. How did *you* like it?"

"I loved it when I was biting you after I woke up. What did you mean you were nervous I'd get addicted? You don't get nervous about anything."

Colnar sighed as I handed him a plate. "Do you remember how I explained to you how much I wanted to meet my mate? I can't alter memories like a vampire, so I just kind of have to disappear until my spell wears off after I've fed on a human. They think they are in love with me and I've had to sneak out the window while they have their phone out booking wedding venues when they were just looking for a one-night stand.

"Other supes get addicted like humans, but they don't start planning weddings and how many children you're going to have. There used to be a time my kind were kept as slaves for other supes because they liked how we made them feel. It was like this big, dirty secret. Everyone was against mixing before the territory wars except the Incubus and Succubae in secret. I know the big romance story with King Raffaele and Queen Meridona was that he captured her hoping to use her as leverage to end the war and fell in love with her singing, but my kind knows the real story.

"Her singing stopped him from raping her, starving

her, and keeping her for a slave. My kind knows exactly what his intent was, even with the story they gave out. Piero, his father, died in battle after getting into a fight with Raffaele about a Succubus he had been taking up with. She wanted to leave because she could tell he was becoming obsessed. Raffaele wanted Piero to *force* her to stay.

"Piero was the one that saved my kind that fate after he started The Order and there were laws passed against it. It broke his heart Raffaele wanted him to bend that rule so he could do that to the poor Succubus. That was how Piero met the final death when we were trying to settle a dispute between the Satyrs and the Fae. He said the wrong thing and a Satyr took his head off.

"I know being with Meridona has changed Raffaele for the better and so has having Aria for a child. I want you to think of the man you know as our king and remember that there was a point in his life he wanted to keep my kind for his pleasure. Raffaele got more protective of our kind after his mate ended up being one of us and his daughter is half.

"It's supposed to be different with your mate. You can enjoy my nature for what it is without becoming obsessive. But in this situation, I don't know what it is. I don't know if I'm meant to share you or this is some trick of Nature, and it's not going to be like that for us. I don't think I can deal with loving you this long, then have you do that to me."

I swallowed my food and put my hand over his. He wasn't putting anything out right then. "You were sending something to me when I bit you. I loved it and definitely want to feel more of it, but I don't feel like I need to control you to get it."

I noticed he was shoveling his food in his face like even though he had given me this speech, he still wanted to fool around. He was already done eating and shoved his plate away with a smirk. My confident Incubus was back.

"So, what do you say, witch? Want to play around with an Incubus?"

"I want to play with my mate, Colnar."

The next thing I knew, Colnar had me off the stool and pressed against the pantry. He moved like a vampire. He had his mouth on my neck and his hand was cupping my breast. I felt his sexual energy gently probing my stomach again, and I practically slumped in his arms.

He had one arm slung behind my back holding me up while he devoured my neck and the other hand was still up my shirt. He said he was worried about me becoming addicted, but he was sending it at me quite strongly.

"Problems, witch?" he growled.

I started to use my magic to push back and let my fangs graze his tongue. He finally pulled back and looked me in the eye. He looked a little surprised.

"I'm not just a witch," I reminded him, my hand going to the bulge in his leather trousers.

"No, you're a sexy hybrid, and I don't think I'm going to make it to the bedroom," Colnar growled.

He spun me around so that my back was to him. The sexual energy was practically pulsing out of him into my back. It was making my knees go weak. Colnar leaned me over the counter a little, and I wondered if he was going to take me right there. I was surprised when he was so gentle as he tugged my shirt and trousers off because his hands were pretty insistent.

His eyes glowed violet when he turned me around

again. I'd never seen them do that before, but it was beautiful. I caressed his cheek and felt the rough stubble there. His eyes traveled up and down my body hungrily.

"Shit," he groaned, adjusting himself.

I didn't even warn him. He probably already knew about it. I let my magic go out my finger as I traced it along his cock. "You can take that out, you know."

His hands went around my waist, and he set me down on the kitchen counter. "No. I've pictured this in my head a hundred times, and I'm not ruining this."

"You pictured this in the kitchen?" I gasped as he kissed my neck.

Colnar didn't answer. His sexual energy was violet, like his eyes, and unlike anything I had seen. I couldn't manipulate it like him, but I could tell what he needed. He needed to please me right now, and he wanted me to give him a few love bites.

While his hands explored my body, I let my fangs prick his shoulder, and then I would lap up the blood. I could tell it excited him, and his blood was like the perfect wine. I sank my fangs in and drank when his fingers suddenly slid inside me. Between his blood, his fingers, and that energy coming off him, I wanted to eat him alive.

He sent this huge wave of energy at me, and my eyes rolled back into my head. I withdrew my fangs and leaned back panting.

"Now I have you where I want you, beloved," Colnar said in a smooth voice.

I've no idea how he did this, but he managed to lower himself to lick my clit *and* free his erection. That man had to have twenty hands at once. He managed to get his trousers to his ankles with his face buried in my pussy.

We hadn't even made it out of the kitchen. I was leaning back on the counter panting and writhing.

Witches and warlocks could see sexual energy and read it, but we couldn't manipulate it or feed off it like an Incubus or Succubus. When I was with a human, it was always red. It just hit me now as the purple energy Colnar was sending at me seemed to caress my entire body at once that it was different colors for all my mates. I hadn't realized or questioned it before now because I was too wrapped up in what we were doing.

A wave of violet energy overwhelmed me, and I pulled Colnar's hair as I came. He kissed his way back up to my mouth and gave me this incorrigible grin.

"Can you handle more, my hybrid?"

Colnar was going to pay for taunting me. I'd become bolder now that I'd been with Jago and Cirrus and I had come to know I had a certain power over all of them that seemed to be augmented by my witch and vampire abilities. Colnar could have disabled every single person on our team that wasn't immune to his Incubus abilities if he sent out enough sexual energy and we both knew that. I already knew Colnar put Quinn's wolf away and according to Cirrus, gender didn't really matter to him.

Colnar needed a little lesson in hybrids. His sexual energy gave me great pleasure, but I wasn't about to become his sex slave or let him use it on me to sway me. I let my eyes trail down his hard chest to his cock. Colnar was teasing me, but I could tell by his straining erection he needed release soon. I finally realized he wasn't teasing me. He was asking permission because he was still worried I'd get addicted and use him.

I was too young to have experienced that part of his history. I had no idea King Raffaele ever wanted to keep a

Succubus captive before one ended up his mate. I needed to ease Colnar's mind. He was standing in front of me with a raging erection in the middle of a storm of sexual energy, and he was vulnerable right now. He had no idea if I would be saying yes to him because I wanted to or because of what he was sending out.

I caressed the rough stubble on his cheek instead of his cock like I originally planned. "What you were told about mates holds true for us. I'm enjoying myself *a lot,* but I'm not going to be like everyone else." I remember what he said to me when I bit him and felt his sexual energy up close when I woke up and needed to heal. I leaned forward and whispered in his ear. "You'll find I like it a little rough, beloved."

Colnar groaned when my fang grazed his ear. He didn't need to be told twice or need any great convincing what he had been told about mates was true. He grabbed my ass and slid me to the edge of the counter. I repeated his words back to him because I just thought that was what he was into.

I was young compared to my mates, but I was old enough to know not to make assumptions about anything in my line of work. He asked my permission, so I was trying to give him permission for what I thought he wanted.

He didn't want, though. He was passionate, but not rough. His thrusts worked me into a frenzy, and the violet cloud around us was practically a tornado. I'd never seen that before, but I'd never been with an Incubus. Colnar had his face buried in my neck, giving me access to his neck.

We were both getting close. My orgasm ripped through me before his did, but it was my fangs in his neck that sent him over the edge. We just stayed there, me sitting on the counter with him buried inside my clutching each other.

Colnar finally started chuckling. "You know, I was sure my sister was lying through her teeth when she said it was different and better with your mate. I went totally out of control and didn't kill you or knock you out."

Colnar scooped me up and started walking towards my bedroom. "I want to explore this mate thing more in a proper bed."

PRESENT DAY

I still hadn't contacted my mates yet, but I'd used their blood to locate them. I periodically did that after I sent them away. They had all gone back home, but often when I checked in on them, they were drunk. The only reason I wasn't drinking away my misery at being away from them was just that I didn't like being drunk. I kept hoping I'd feel them go back to Switzerland and The Order, but over the last few years, they still hadn't.

The only reason I hadn't contacted them yet was that Rainer finally told me where I had gone wrong with my spell and what needed to happen so no one would kill anyone when we were marking each other. Rainer's goblet seemed so obvious I should have figured it out myself. Mine was too generic.

What Rainer and I were trying to figure out was the combination of herbs to go in the goblet once we mixed our blood together. The wolfsbane would work for Quinn as it did for Ronric and I already knew Silver Jasmine was what was needed for Cirrus.

Jago told me during our week together that dragons used Wineberry for healing and that pregnant dragons ate it to help with their eggs. Rainer just nodded and agreed to try to find it when I told him. It wasn't a common plant and was probably only grown in dragon territories now.

Aria and I both thought Hellebore was the correct herb for Colnar. I had no idea he was doing this until he told me during our week alone, but apparently, the Incubus and Succubus could delay their feedings if they crushed it and put it into a drink. Aria had experience with it because apparently, Cade put some stupid rules in his contract with her and Colnar admitted to taking it because after he started having feelings for me, he didn't want to feed on anyone else.

That just left me. It was almost a unanimous agreement that the herb they used for Aria wouldn't work for me. We weren't the same type of hybrid, and that particular herb seemed to be special to her. Kalon liked to wax poetic about how her eyes were that shade of blue because of the Sapphire Seed her mother took while pregnant with her and they would all get distracted.

There was no herb I could think of that I had any reaction to like most supe species did. I was going to have to call my mother about anything that might have helped her while she was pregnant with me. There had to be something since hybrid births were always hard. I knew my mother always said she had it easy with me compared to other mothers of hybrids because my witch side didn't have her feed off anything against her nature, but surely, she had some difficulty.

I reached out to my mother telepathically. She started in on me right away without even asking what I wanted.

"*Liliana? When are we going to get a visit from our only child? I think you are avoiding us. Your father says he can feel your aura sometimes and you feel wretched. Tell your mother what's going on.*"

"*Mother, I'll tell you when I have good news. I'm working on something, and the light is finally shining through. I need your help.*"

"*Do you need me to kill someone? Tell me who hurt you, and I'll rip their head off.*"

"*Mother, no. I'm working on a spell. And I can take care of myself if someone hurts me. I need to know if there was anything you took while you were pregnant with me that helped.*"

"*Nature help me, Liliana, if you're pregnant, someone is going to die. You haven't even met your mate yet! Tell me it's not some filthy human. Raffaele will have your head for that.*"

"*Mother! I'm not pregnant. I need an herb that is special to me for a spell. I'm way too careful to get pregnant by anyone, human or supe.*"

"*And just who are you having sex with, Liliana?*" my mother demanded.

"*No one! I'm just telling you I'm not pregnant. Can you remember anything you took that helped?*"

"*I heard about what happened to Raffaele's daughter. You be honest with me, young lady. Are you asking me about special herbs because you're in the same situation? And you never told us? Your father would have found the answer. Is it someone we know?*"

I groaned. My mother never missed a thing and to be honest, I was surprised she hadn't already reached out to me to ask if she had already heard about Aria. She must have literally just found out.

"*Yes, Mother and you know all of them. My bodyguards. Are you going to help me or fuss?*"

"And not a proper vampire in the bunch. Your little witchy side was making me need more blood. To the point, I would have hurt your father. The midwife treating me was Fae, and the only thing that stopped your magic from giving me raging blood thirst was Fairymoss. Your eyes ended up the same greenish-brown color of the Fairymoss tea I drank. Maybe you were just destined to end up with a fairy. You couldn't have picked a vampire too if you had to have more than one?"

I pinched the bridge of my nose with my fingers, glad my mother couldn't see my face. She ended up mates with a warlock, and I knew she loved me as I was, but she was quite proud of being a vampire. Before I ended up in the Ottoman Empire that fateful day Xenon rescued me and recruited me into The Order, once I was old enough, my mother kept throwing vampires at me hoping one would end up being my mate.

"I didn't have any say in my mates. Nature picked them just like she did with you and my father. I had no idea my body-guards were going to end up being my mates when I chose them to put a vampire in the mix."

"Well, you should have had a vampire as a bodyguard just on principle."

"Mother, I don't need a vampire as a bodyguard because I've got that part covered."

"You're right, dear. Your mates are lovely. I take it since you're working on a spell, nothing is sealed yet. When you've sorted everything, bring everyone home, and we'll have a party like nothing we've had before."

"Thank you, mother. And I'll visit once I've got everything figured out."

I sighed and rubbed my forehead. Not only was I going to have to convince my mates to come back, but Jago was also going to have to bring Wineberry and

Cirrus was going to have to bring Fairymoss for this to work. Rainer and I couldn't exactly portal into dragon or Fae territory and start asking around where we could find those ingredients.

It wasn't during my time, but back when there were more dragons, the discarded eggshells and mother dragons that died in birth were coveted for their parts in spells. I knew from my time in The Order Piero outlawed those spells even before dragons almost became extinct. It had been the law for a long time now, but the few remaining dragons would remember and not take well to a witch and warlock showing up in their territory.

Fae territory was cloaked and hard to find, much like The Order headquarters. I knew how to get there because I'd visited with Cirrus on missions, but *no one* went to Fae territory without a Fae escort. You'd get an arrow through your eye in seconds.

I let Rainer know what ingredients we needed, and he agreed it would be best to let Cirrus and Jago get what we needed or either bring me back with them to acquire it. We still needed to make the goblet and had been putting that off because the herb situation was taking so long.

Rainer portalled out to Infinity Coven territory to have the goblet made after I gave him everyone's sigils. Soon, I'd have everything I needed. I couldn't put off the difficult conversations I knew I needed to have much longer. And I didn't think I could anymore. I wanted them back more than anything now that I knew I could have all of them.

5 YEARS AGO

Being with Colnar for a week was amazing. For an Incubus, he seemed to like cuddling a lot. He'd snuggle into my shoulder and rub his nose in my neck. He finally told me he never actually got to cuddle with anyone before and he always wanted to. He always had to make a quick exit after sex because of the reactions everyone had to his energy. The other Incubus and Succubus he had been with just wanted to feed and leave.

We still had plenty of mind-blowing sex, but Colnar seemed to get the most joy at either holding me or me holding him. I liked that part too. His violet energy was like this comforting hug, kind of like magic could be when we just laid in bed snuggling. Like Jago and Cirrus, I was sad to see him go.

Quinn practically broke the door down when it was his turn. Colnar and I were just sitting on the couch holding each other again, and Quinn was early. He must have gotten tired of waiting. Colnar just scowled.

"You're interrupting my time, you mangy wolf."

"Give over. I'm only ten minutes early!"

"*My* ten minutes," Colnar snapped. "You couldn't wait outside ten minutes? You're such an infant."

"Colnar," I said gently. "I think you forget I'm younger than Quinn and that insults me too. Quinn is only ten minutes early, and he's been waiting for the longest. Can you forgive him for being a little early?"

"Only for you, beloved. The Lycan can eat dick. Your wolf can't compare to what I can give her," Colnar growled on the way out.

Quinn looked like he was about to jump out of his skin. He took a running start, leapt over the back of the sofa, and buried his nose in my neck. I could tell his wolf was scenting me. We'd already done this ages ago so he could always find me and I had no idea why he was doing it again.

"You smell like vanilla and cedarwood with spices. My wolf liked your scent when I was just scenting you to find you, but now he just wants to be close to it."

"Quinn, since we don't know how this is supposed to work, are you going to be able to control him and not claim me and mark me this week?"

"Liliana, it's been hell for my wolf and me these past weeks waiting my turn and knowing what you were doing. I've been worried this entire time you'd pick before I got my chance with you. My wolf will behave because neither of us wants to ruin things. Jago didn't acknowledge you?"

"No, and you can't claim me either until we figure out what Nature intended when she did this. I'm not sure if I'm supposed to be spending all this time with you and it's my decision, or I'll have to rely on a spell to tell me. Colnar and Cirrus seem to be okay with the idea of sharing, though I'm doubting that after Colnar's reaction to you getting here early. I know it's not in you or Jago's nature to share, so there's something I'm missing."

Quinn still had his face buried in my neck sniffing my hair. It was starting to tickle. "I've had three weeks to wait and plan this week, and now I have no idea what I want to do with you."

"Tell me about your plans, and we'll go from there?"

"Well, I just want to kiss you first. But not on the sofa. In my bed."

So far, everyone had wanted to go to my bed, not theirs. They'd all decorated their rooms in all my various villas so differently. Their rooms all fit their species and personalities. Quinn tried to make his room look as much as the outdoors as possible. He picked the room with the most windows and painted the walls a sage green. He had several plants everywhere, but he also loved luxury. He wouldn't sleep in a bed without percale sheets and a down comforter, and I knew he had gel mattresses in every room that was his.

"So, take me to your bedroom, Quinn."

Quinn scooped me up like I weighed nothing and went bounding down the hall with me bouncing in his arms. He practically kicked the door open and flung us both on the bed. Quinn was ravenous as he kissed my neck. I could feel the rough stubble on his chin growing a little like his wolf was poking through.

I gently shoved his shoulders away, and I was looking at amber eyes. His canines weren't out yet. That was a good sign. "Quinn, your wolf," I reminded him. "Don't do anything you'll regret."

"I can control my wolf. He wants to come out and play, but I'm keeping him at bay. You're safe, Liliana. I won't claim you or mark you until you say it's okay."

His amber eyes were sparkling with mischief, and I wondered exactly what he wanted to do. "Well, you said you wanted to kiss me, and you haven't yet."

Quinn let out a little growl and wasn't exactly gentle when he kissed me. Quinn always seemed to have some sort of scruff on his face. He'd come to breakfast after a shower like he'd shaved, but almost as soon as we'd finished eating, he already had a five o'clock shadow. The burn of his stubble against my chin was exciting me, and I let my fang prick his tongue.

Quinn all but tore my shirt off as I sucked on his tongue. None of my other mates ripped at my clothes like this, and it made me want to flip this sexy wolf on his back and furiously ride him. I tried, but Quinn wasn't having any of it.

He pinned my arms down, and that was when I saw his canines were out. He looked down at my ripped shirt and growled again. He ripped my bra in two *with his teeth*. Nature help me, I wanted him to fuck me right that minute as rough as possible. I felt this canines and stubble as he nipped and nuzzled my breasts.

My arms were totally pinned by my head, and I couldn't touch him if I wanted to, but I needed his cock right now. I lifted my hips and started grinding myself against his erection. He threw his head back and howled. When his amber eyes came down to meet mine, they were wild this time, and I was starting to wonder if I'd poked his wolf a little too much.

"Mine!" Quinn roared, lowering his head to kiss my neck again. He kissed his way down to my breast and yelled *mine* again. He was rough when he yanked my skirt up to my waist and pulled my thong off. He looked down

at me with my shirt and bra destroyed and my skirt bunched up at my waist.

The only thing Quinn seemed capable of saying right now was just to roar *mine* over and over. He gave my body an appreciative look before he mounted me and slid into me. The sex was rough, feral. If Quinn was only capable of grunting *mine,* I wasn't capable of doing anything except clawing his back now that he'd released my hands and scream his name.

I bit him pretty hard on the shoulder when I came, enjoying the explosion of his blood in my mouth as my body was wracked with pleasure. Quinn didn't last much longer. He screamed *mine* one last time before throwing back his head and howling as his seed spilled into me.

Quinn seemed to go back to normal, and his ability to speak full sentences came back as he stayed on top of me nuzzling my neck again.

"Quinn?" I asked, petting his back. "What was all that *mine* business about?"

Quinn just chuckled. "Did it scare you? Wolves get possessive. I suppose I just wanted to yell it loud enough that the other three heard me. Me *and* my wolf are going to fight for you. We don't care if we have to fight a dragon, a Fae, and an Incubus. We will find a way for Nature to make us your true mate if we have to fight Nature too. I will spend this week romancing you and giving you every reason to pick me. I want you begging me to claim you and mark you."

"Quinn," I said, going to play with his long hair. "I don't want to hurt any of you. I don't know why Nature chose all four of you instead of just one of you. You knew I was in love with Xenon. I have to think this is some sort of curse and we're all going to be hurt. Before we left for that speech, I tried to commune with Nature and ask her to rid me of my feelings with Xenon. Maybe she thought I was egotistical asking her to get involved in my love life, so she did this to put me in my place."

"Oh, Liliana," Quinn said, finally starting to sound like himself. "There's an answer to this. Nature does everything for a reason, and she only punishes when you do something that comes with a price. Xenon has a mate and never could have returned your feelings. He and his mate are pretty fertile and have several children now. You were totally justified in asking for a little help moving on."

"Someone, if not all of us, will be hurt, Quinn."

"I'm the last one of us you have to entertain for a week. Commune with Nature again and use your magic. The answer will come to you like it always does."

A ria and I were sitting on the sofa with Ronric while we waited for Rainer to come back with the Goblet the Infinity Coven made. I had been thinking about my time alone with each man and what Ronric said about Quinn claiming me like a pup. After I told Ronric about how Quinn kept screaming *mine* over and over, he just rolled his eyes.

"Sorry, Liliana. That was definitely him claiming you like a horny pup. It's usually much more beautiful than that, and there's a speech that goes with it. Please tell me your dragon did a little better."

I wasn't mad at Quinn. He hadn't centered his wolf and didn't know he was doing it. "At least the sex was really good," I said, shrugging.

Aria snorted. "Lycans are fun in bed, aren't they?"

Ronric grabbed Aria and playfully pulled her into his lap. He planted a huge kiss on her neck. "This little wench wanted to play with my wolf like a toy the night I claimed her."

"Are you insane?" I asked. A feral Lycan was deadly,

and he could have just marked her right then and there. None of us knew what would happen if we didn't mark each other together.

"I asked her the same thing. She drew my wolf out and turned him into a puppy," he said, laughing.

It looked like she was about to answer, but Kalon came running in the room screaming. He had been hanging out in the hot tub while we were chatting. He ran out stark naked and dripping wet, yelling to turn the television on. I wondered exactly how many of Aria's mates I was going to see naked or half naked before I got mine here.

Aria was closest and flipped the TV on, asking what channel. We were all shocked to see that little toad man Aleksei in front of a huge crowd talking about Zimin. We thought World War III ended with Zimin's death. There weren't any witches or warlocks helping anyone in his circle anymore as far as we knew.

The toad man was up in front of a huge crowd back in Russia trying to rally a crowd. We all knew from Aria's intel that Zimin meant to take Turkey, then Syria and Afghanistan. I'd already ruined his plans for Turkey. My parents weren't in The Order, but they divided their time between Turkey and Syria, spending most of their time in Syria.

I'd already warned them, and my mother was itching for someone to bring war back to my birthplace so she could be a warrior again. My father was no slouch with battle magic either for a diplomat. He was capable of hexing an entire battalion without breaking a sweat. Let Aleksei try to continue on with Zimin's plans where my parents lived.

Aleksei was trying to rally a bigger army in Russia by

blaming Syria for Zimin's death. Aleksei and Zimin would have thought their plans to take Turkey was successful. Their plants were all my puppets now and spies. I hadn't checked in with them because I thought Zimin's revolution would die with him.

We all just looked at each other. Aria sighed. "You're the boss. Do you want me here or do you want me in Russia working Aleksei like the original plan was when Zimin was alive?"

"Actually, The Order tribunal is our boss, and I'm shocked they haven't contacted any of us. I'm pretty sure I know why they haven't contacted me, but all of you were instrumental in stopping this. Let me contact Xenon and find out what's up."

Almost as soon as I reached out to Xenon telepathically, a portal opened up in my living room, and he appeared. He crossed his arms and gave me the same look my father gave me when I had done something wrong.

"Why haven't you sorted this mate situation out yet, Liliana? You have the answers."

"I think World War III trumps my personal issues, Xenon," I snapped. "Is there another coven we need to be looking at?"

"Do I need to go work the ugly little man?" Aria asked, wrinkling her nose.

"The ugly little man will die soon. The Order didn't want to bother any of you during this trying time and because we worried you'd be too distracted to—"

"Excuse me?" Aria snapped. "You had no problem with all of us together when Zimin was alive."

"And now that he's not, you can rest and be with your mates. Liliana can sort things with hers. We've got another vampire close to Aleksei. One that fits his personal tastes in women. She's already compelled him and gotten the information we needed. Zimin's inner circle all had documents they were only supposed to open if he was killed. They were supposed to take up his cause, and they would have outside help. They would be given great power. They think if they carry the torch, they'll be blessed. We've got this covered."

"Can I kill Aleksei?" Aria asked, bouncing in Ronric's lap. Kalon was still naked and dripping on my hardwood floors. "I staked him out when I thought he was my next mark and he's a pig."

"No, because you're going to do it like it's still the human Dark Ages," Xenon said. Aria was pouting. "They all meet in a conference room in an empty building in the middle of the night in Saint Petersburg. We've scoped out the ventilation system, and we can get them all in one go with poison gas."

"Where the fun in *that?*" Aria asked.

"It's not fun. It's safe and effective."

I could tell Xenon wanted to say more, but another portal opened, and Rainer walked through. He eyed Kalon and rolled his eyes.

"Can't you and Ronric ever keep your clothes on?"

"You're not that great at keeping your clothes on yourself, warlock," Ronric boomed.

"Rainer, love, we were just watching the news. Zimin's cronies are trying to keep World War III going, but Xenon won't let us play," Aria said.

Xenon's cool exterior looked like it was slipping for once. "Because all four of you need Order training and I don't think you realize this has been going on for five years for Liliana and her mates. Liliana needs to end this for all their sakes so they can all be happy and get back to work if that's what they decide."

Aria's eyes were glowing red and Ronric's gold. She told me about how Xenon always made her want to bite him. The diplomat in me came out before she totally maimed him.

"I'll contact my mates. How about you do the take-down on the conference room via video so Aria and the others can see how we do things?"

Xenon shot me a grateful look, nodded, and disappeared. Aria just nestled into Ronric's chest.

"There's just something about that warlock that makes me want to maim him."

"He saved my life, remember, *dragoste?*" Kalon asked.

Aria grabbed a pillow off the sofa and launched it at Kalon like she'd only just noticed he was butt naked. "Put some clothes on, you naughty vampire."

"You know you love my ass," Kalon said, shaking it at us as he dripped back to their bedroom to change.

"Now that the naked vampire is gone, here's the goblet, Liliana," Rainer said, handing it over to me.

His goblet was different than mine. I could feel the power pulsing from it. I already knew I was going to have to put on a show with it so they could see they were my mates.

Now, I just needed to contact them.

5 YEARS AGO

I had so much fun with my time alone with my mates. I wasn't even thinking about what was going to happen when we were all together again. We didn't just spend the entire week having sex, though I did a lot of that with all of them. There was also a lot of eating, laughing, talking, and just holding each other being goofy.

As I watched Quinn sleep, I wondered how I hadn't noticed what was right in front of me this entire time. I'd been so hung up on Xenon and worried about ruining a working relationship. I didn't even try to explore dating any of them. I was starting to think if I hadn't been so stupid and stubborn for hundreds of years, I'd know which one of them was supposed to be mine.

I still didn't have the answer, and I was closer to all of them than I'd been before. None of them jumped out at me as being *the one*. There was some young, stupid part of me that remembered the stories my father told me before bed and one of them would kiss me, and I'd just know. Bells would start ringing, and the entire room would smell of flowers. I'd just *know*.

I felt like that with every single one of them. It was like every sound in the room was amplified, and I could smell the fragrant flowers in the garden when they kissed me. I smiled down at Quinn like him snoring was the cutest thing I'd ever seen and heard.

I smiled at him because I was coming up with a plan. This had to be some sort of test for me. They all felt right, and I couldn't tell from their blood because I was supposed to use magic to figure this out. I had to write the spell of my life. It had to pick who my true mate was and do it in a way that didn't hurt the others. I knew thinking I could write a spell that wouldn't totally ruin our working relationship was probably too much to ask, but I was going to try.

I was supposed to have more time with Quinn. The others were supposed to come back for lunch, and I was naïve enough to believe nothing bad would happen. I felt them before I heard them. Drinking that much of their blood must have deepened our connection. I could tell Jago, Cirrus, and Colnar were standing outside the front door, and I could already feel from the irritating buzz of their auras they were fighting.

I eased myself away from Quinn and threw a robe on. Quinn was exhausted. We were up late having sex, and I could tell he wanted to keep going. He asked if we could just stop and hold each other because he was struggling with his wolf. Quinn didn't meet my eyes when he admitted if we kept going, he was going to mark me without my permission. I just dragged him to bed and played with his hair until he fell asleep. I tried to soothe

the wolf that kept poking out more and more the longer we were together.

I threw open the front door, and Cirrus and Jago were shoving each other. Colnar was threatening both of them with a huge blast of sexual energy if they ruined my morning and kept reminding them they were early. They finally noticed me standing there staring with my arms crossed and an eyebrow cocked.

I didn't comment on them being early. They were already here, and I wasn't going to send them away. "Have all of you eaten?" I asked. They were supposed to be here for lunch, and when I looked at the antique clock by the door, it was only seven in the morning.

My dragon had the nerve to look sheepish. "No. None of us have. We've been going crazy, and I don't think any of us slept last night knowing we'd get to see you today."

Colnar just breezed past me and lounged on the sofa like a sex god. "The wolf needed a little payback. He was early for his time too," Colnar smirked.

"Perhaps all of you are not aware of this, or you are and have just forgotten," I said, putting them in their place and trying to stop any fights before they started. "I know every spell to neutralize all of you. If you start fighting, I'll put you to sleep and let you sleep it off wherever you land."

Cirrus groaned. "You're so sexy when you're mean."

"Stop looking at my treasure like that or I'll rip your balls off and feed them to you." Jago's dragon was rumbling again, and it wasn't the happy noise he had with me.

"She's *not* your treasure, she's *mine,*" Quinn growled from the door. He was panting, and his wolf was half out.

I already knew my eyes were glowing, so I called my magic to my hands and let it spark. "Do the four of you really want to do this right now? You're ruining anything I enjoyed while I was with you. Can we just eat like we used to and have fun?"

"The fairy needs to put his boner away before I bite it off with very sharp teeth," Jago rumbled even louder. He was starting to shake the windows and paintings on the wall.

"Jago!" I warned, letting the magic in my hands erupt in more white sparks. "If you don't put your dragon away and stop threatening people, I'm going to zap you, and you won't like it as much as my bite. That goes for you too, Quinn. Put your wolf away. Cirrus, try to contain yourself and Colnar, wipe that smirk off your face. I want a totally *normal* breakfast. Can all of you manage that without ruining our weeks together?"

Cirrus was biting his lip like me ordering them around was the sexiest thing he'd ever seen. Colnar definitely noticed it too and it wasn't helping that smirk I told him to get rid of. Jago and Quinn were both working on their breathing to put their beasts away before I put it away for them.

I stared at them with my eyebrow cocked. They all seemed to have calmed down, so I stalked off to the kitchen to cook. Cirrus came up behind me and put his hand on my shoulder. I heard a few muffled growls and rumbles behind me.

"May I?" he said, holding up a bag.

I held my breath. I had no idea what was going to happen if I said Cirrus could cook. Colnar decided to save my ass.

"I, for one, would love some Fae food."

Cirrus scowled, and that was when I realized he intended to only cook for me, and the others could just figure out their own food situation. Cirrus was right next to me, and I knew everyone had enhanced hearing and would hear if I whispered. I spoke to him telepathically instead so we could have some privacy.

"Cirrus, please. This is not like our week together, and we aren't alone anymore. Things need to be like how they were before we were mates. You cooked for all of us before."

"Not Fae food. They don't deserve it."

"Cirrus, you sound like a snob. Either you cook for everyone, or you don't cook at all."

"Yes, Mistress."

Mistress? That was new. I watched him adjust his erection and set off cooking. I sat at the counter with my mates, and they were all eyeing each other suspiciously. Normally, our breakfast was spent with laughter and playful banter, but that seemed to be gone now. I missed it, but I knew I was an idiot to hope we could go back to that. I tried to talk about work instead.

"Any news from Xenon?" I asked.

Jago's eyes flashed green and gold. "Why? Do you miss him?"

I sighed. "No, I'm just thinking about work. There is a war going on."

"Use your nose, wanker," Quinn snapped. "Her scent doesn't change when she mentions his name anymore. She's pissed, not thinking about him."

"I'll rip your childish spine out, you—"

"Enough!" I yelled. "War, remember?"

"Liliana," Colnar said. "While everyone is already angry, I might as well bring up something you forget now that we are together. I've been taking Hellebore while you were with the others, but I *have* to feed a certain way. I don't want to feed off anyone else. I don't think I can. Do you understand where I'm going with this? I'm not like the others. I understand that if you do this with me, I have to deal with it while you do it with the others too."

I understood where Colnar was coming from, but Jago and Quinn didn't. Cirrus was already yelling, and Quinn and Jago had their beasts out again. I had a naturally low, throaty speaking voice and didn't raise it often. I didn't need to. Even when I was with yelling politicians, I never yelled or raised my voice.

Clearly, my mates needed a little schooling. I let my magic pool into my pointer finger and placed it to my throat. This would amplify my voice. "Stop it, now!" I yelled, my voice shaking the windows. "This is what is going to happen. I think all of you can get it through your thick skulls. Colnar *has* to have sex with me to survive, and I want to feed him. I think you all understand I *want* to be with all of you too.

"Unlike before, where you all had a week with me, this is how it's going to be. Understand, I hate this too. Since none of you can behave when we're together, we're going to work out a schedule. There will be one day a week where we're alone, two days a week where we're all together, and one day a week where I'm totally alone working with magic trying to figure this mess out."

Jago crinkled his nose. "Why don't you take three days to figure it out so I don't have to spend time with these assholes? The fairy reeks every time he pops a boner when you get bossy, and Colnar's vibes give me the creeps."

I cocked an eyebrow at Jago. I was wondering how

many of my mates were a little bisexual and could be affected by Colnar. I already knew Quinn was because Colnar put his wolf away. Cirrus flat out told me. Apparently, Jago wasn't at all.

"I don't like being around Colnar either when he's not focusing his aim," Quinn said. "I still don't know what happened when I was injured."

I thought everyone was going to give Quinn a hard time. Especially Colnar, but Colnar didn't even smirk. "Easy. It was the hexes. I figured it out after we woke up and they told us the hexes messed with our nature. I *think* you and Liliana both felt me because I was sending out both Incubus *and* Succubus vibes because the hex was still starting. You can be secure in your masculinity, wolf. An Incubus didn't best your wolf. As for you, Cirrus, I've been to Fae parties before."

"Oh, shut up, you filthy Incubus," Cirrus snapped.

"That's not what your sister said when I was fucking her."

I flung my wrist and set a magical barrier between Cirrus and Colnar. Colnar finally stopped grinning when he saw the look on my face. "*Really,* Colnar? You know what this situation is right now and you really want to goad Cirrus like that? All of you get out. Today is my day with Cirrus. Get your shit together and figure out a schedule. And before any of you open your mouth, we are all having two days together because all of you need to learn to get along again. Think of it like Order training. You're back in the equivalent of supe kindergarten where you learn to share and play nice. Get it? Now get the hell out my house."

PRESENT DAY

We were all over the place, and I was a little pissed at Xenon. Now that I had all the ingredients, I was ready to contact my mates. The last thing I needed to do was figure out the order I was going to contact them in. Xenon portalled into my living room while I was discussing that with Aria, Ronric, Rainer, and Kalon.

"What is it?" I snapped.

Xenon looked surprised at my tone. "I thought everyone would want to know what we've discovered in Unseen Moon territory and with Aleksei. Was I wrong?"

"No, proceed," I said, hoping he would hurry up.

"There was a failsafe in the event Cade was ever caught. It's filthy blood magic, and it's outlawed. He split his pith and put it into at least two totems. One was in Unseen Moon territory, and we think Aleksei has the other. Zimin always had it, and it passed to Aleksei with his notes. Cade is still moving pieces from Tartarus. Except this time, his goal was also to get out of the Underworld."

Kalon snorted. "He made Horcruxes?"

We all looked at him like he had a second head. I knew about the magic Cade had done, but that wasn't what it was called.

"What?" Kalon asked innocently. "Harry Potter? None of you like human fiction? Seriously? That was all humans were talking about for a while. I had to read it and watch the movies to see what the fuss was about. I thought the little witch school was a good idea for us. It was cute. Why are you all staring at me?"

Kalon had to be the only supe I knew who had dipped his toes in human supernatural fiction. I found a lot of human literature and television shows to be very interesting, but I steered clear of anything with witches, vampires, or anything personal to me.

Aria seemed to think it was adorable. She tackled Kalon and started nipping at his neck. "Please tell me you didn't do that *Twilight* series too."

"Yes! Twilight!" Kalon laughed, tickling Aria. "Everything about vampires and Lycans is totally wrong. One day, I will tie you down and force you to watch it. None of you like reading human stories about us?"

Kalon seemed shocked none of us shared his interest. Xenon cleared his throat. "Well, it's not called whatever you just said, but we still have a problem. We destroyed one totem, but we need to get the one Aleksei has. Pith Totems are filthy magic and can cause all sorts of trouble. We need to end this war and stop Aleksei from taking anything Cade says too far."

"I take it you're in need of my particular set of skills again?" Aria asked.

Xenon's easy smile came back. "All four of you. Nature fated you to be together for a reason. Aria, you can get close to Aleksei to get close to the totem, but Rainer will have to destroy it. And who better to clear out anyone who would want to pick up Aleksei's torch than Ronric and Kalon?"

Xenon was being a manipulative shit, and he wasn't usually like that. He was kissing their asses, and he wasn't saying all that needed to be said. I didn't even let Rainer mention the little tidbit Xenon left out.

"Were you going to kiss a little more ass before you brought up it takes more than one witch to destroy a Pith Totem? It's also going to take more than Ronric and Kalon to clear out a compound. Say what you are leaving out, Xenon."

Xenon gave me this cheeky wink, and I was starting to see why Aria said he always made her want to bite him. There would have been a time a wink like that would have melted my heart, but now it was just irritating me.

"I never could bullshit you, Liliana. The Order wants to see what two hybrids can do as a team now that we have you. It's time hybrids come together instead of being told to avoid each other for your safety. We want you to fix this mate situation of yours so you can finally be happy and we want all of you working *together.*"

I cocked an eyebrow at him and wondered if this was a test. When he was training me so long ago, there were frequent unannounced tests. Did he want me to compel the answer out of him?

Xenon held up his hands in surrender. Maybe it wasn't a test. "I know we've had you in politics. Cirrus and Jago always reported that you kept up your fight training and have become skilled with several weapons. I think we both know The Lethal Shadow has been craving a little payback since that magic bomb. Your mates probably want a piece of the action too."

I eyed Xenon. He wasn't wrong. I'd just settled myself that I'd always be running countries and not fighting for so long, I never thought I'd personally be able to exact revenge for that little magic bomb. I was tasked with getting the Sorrow Leaves out of Cade's system as soon as possible when we had him in a Hellfire Cage waiting for Aria to get him. I thought my only revenge for that magic bomb was being as rough as possible with the needle and watching Cade barf and shit all over the place while he rapidly detoxed.

"You're actually going to let me fight?" I asked, thinking he had other intentions. I thought he was going to give me orders to let everyone else handle the fighting and go straight for the Pith Totem and destroy it.

Xenon grinned at me. "Well, according to Cirrus and Jago, you've got your choice of weapons. Cirrus reports you're as good as a Fae with the staff, Jago said you're good with the dagger, you've mastered battle magic, and I trained you on the sword myself. The Order would *prefer* if we just took them out at once with the gas like our original plan, but the Pith Totem is in Aleksei's personal quarters. We either need Liliana or Aria to get the combination to the safe from him, and if all of them end up dead, we don't know if someone else will grab the totem and carry on the cause."

Aria just laughed and hugged me. "You mean you're going to let us fight the fun way instead of with machine guns and flamethrowers like you did with Zimin?"

Xenon's brow furrowed. I don't think he was quite used to Aria yet. "We used a sniper rifle on Zimin," Xenon said like he didn't quite get Aria's statement.

Apparently, Aria felt the same way about sniper rifles as she did about cell phones. "Sniper rifles are so impersonal. You want to look your enemy in the eye before you kill them."

Xenon looked utterly flabbergasted, and he always seemed to know what to say before he met Aria and her mates. I think between Kalon's love of human fiction and Aria's insistence on getting up close, and personal for her kills, Xenon didn't know what he had gotten himself into when he finally agreed to my demands that they be asked to join.

Kalon was the closest to Aria. He pulled her in his lap and nipped at her neck. "Not everyone is as deadly in battle as The Sapphire Scythe and needs to use guns."

Xenon looked so relieved Kalon explained that to her he hadn't even realized Kalon insulted him and the majority of The Order that did fight with guns. I snorted because I was trying to hold in my laughter. It seemed like I hadn't laughed in years since I sent my mates away. It seemed like everyone realized Kalon had insulted Xenon *except* Xenon and pretty soon, we were all laughing.

Xenon looked at all of us like we were insane. He cleared his throat. "Yes, can I expect this mate situation dealt with within the next two days and the Pith Totem destroyed?"

I just nodded. Maybe that was my problem. I'd been dragging ass and moping for more reasons than just sending my mates away. I *needed* to work, and Xenon benched me after the magic bomb went off. Xenon only started giving me simple tasks after Aria's intel told us how Zimin was manipulating governments and Zimin was about to come to my backyard.

Even then, I was told to help Aria with the mate situation and do simple things like turning Zimin's plants instead of real work. I was ready to get back to work, even if it wasn't this new mission. I was ready to be back in The Order with my mates by my side again.

Xenon said two days, then move in on Aleksei. I was doing this as soon as Xenon left.

PRESENT DAY

X enon had known me longer than anyone in the room. I was starting to think he had been clueless for hundreds of years about my little crush because he seemed clueless now that I wanted him the fuck out my villa so I could get my damned mates back. After we stopped laughing at him, he seemed just to want to sit there and shoot the shit about his new grandchild. Normally, I would have loved to talk about the arrival of a new hybrid, but I had shit to do.

I finally interrupted him when he started going on and on about being excited about all the shit diapers he was going to have to change. I was excited about a new hybrid, but I couldn't say I liked babies. They kind of grossed me out.

"Xenon, you know I love you, but can you please leave? I need to commune with Nature and get my mates back."

Xenon shook his head to rid himself of his baby induced stupid. "Oh, yes. Sorry. I just love babies. I'll get out your hair."

As soon as he portalled out of my living room, Aria turned to me. "I've been thinking about this, but I'm not sure if it'll work. Hybrid power, right? I can dream walk and you can't, but you can channel me. What if we go to your garden and you channel my gifts when you contact them? I *think* you can contact all of them at once instead of picking an order *and* if you're channeling me, you can send them a little sexual energy as I can so they calm their shit when you reach them."

"Are you sure you don't have some witch blood in there?" I said, grinning at her. "That would actually work."

"I know," she said, winking at me. "I don't just fuck the brains out my warlock mate. We talk too. Now, let's get out to your garden and get *your* mates back."

"I'll need to commune with Nature for a bit before I channel you and reach out to them," I reminded her as we walked outside. I didn't know how much Rainer had told her about witchcraft.

All of my villas had ornate gardens with magical herbs, enchanted trees, and spell infused totems for protection. I needed them to commune with Nature. Quinn needed the gardens to center his wolf, and the Fae also used enchanted gardens. There were several herbs and plants here that Cirrus cultivated. Some wouldn't grow in certain climates, but I had a wide array of Fae and witch plants here whose fragrance perfumed the air.

Aria trailed behind me silently to the stone circle on the ground. It was similar to the pentagram used now, but the glyph for witches and warlocks in the old tongue was in the middle. The old tongue was long gone by the time I was born, but I was still taught in my lessons growing up and could read and speak it fluently.

I sat in the center of the circle. Aria didn't join me just yet because she understood I needed answers from Nature first. I needed to ask Nature for the right things to say to my mates when I did have them all together. She might not have given me the answer the million times I asked her who my mate was, but surely, she would answer now.

I sat in the circle and put myself in a trance. In my trance, I was in a garden similar to the one I was in now, but there was a swirling mist around me, and the enchanted trees were more twisted and their leaves purple and blue, something we couldn't do in real life. I pulled a wood flute out my pocket and started playing the tune every little witch and warlock were taught was Nature's favorite.

Nature never spoke to you directly. She showed you images. They could be past images, and sometimes, she'd show you images of possible futures, but it was up to you to make that future come true. Nature sometimes showed you riddles. Nature could be a fickle master sometimes.

As I finished my tune on the wood flute, I felt my aura tingling as Nature came into my trance. I left my mind open for what she wanted to show me. I tried to keep my groan to myself when I realized what she decided to show me. She didn't need to show me this. This was a day that was forever etched in my memory, and I didn't think I would ever forget.

It had been three years since Nature marked us mates. I'd asked Nature for the answer several times, and she showed me a goblet every time. I'd gone through millions of goblets that didn't do a damned thing. I'd created them from every enchanted tree in my garden. I tried the glyphs for their species. I tried their house sigils. They'd slashed their palms and added their blood to countless goblets and waited as anxiously as I did for something to light up and tell us the answer. Every single goblet was a dud.

We'd been doing the same thing for three years. I'd spend one day alone with each of them. We spent one day all together where I tried anything I could to get them to get along. I'd end up having to send them away before lunch before one of them killed someone. I'd spend two days alone communing with Nature asking for an answer with this goblet and getting nothing.

We were all sitting around my ritual table again. We'd slashed our palm and added our blood. Once again, the goblet did nothing. Jago lost it.

"Nature is playing games! The goblet is not the way. You belong with me, Liliana!"

"She can't even have dragon babies with you, shit head!" Colnar snapped. "You can't please her like I can."

"You're a bottom feeder, Incubus. She belongs with a Fae."

Quinn stood up and just roared *mine* again. When they started doing this, that seemed to be all he was capable of saying. They'd all shoved their chairs back and were screaming. Quinn's wolf was already out, and Jago's dragonhide was starting to form. Cirrus pulled his battle staff out his pocket and tapped it, so it sprang into its full form. I could see a violet cloud surrounding Colnar. He was summoning sexual energy to use it as a weapon.

Over the last two years, they'd taunted and said horrible things to each other, but this was the first time they'd resorting to pulling weapons. I'd had to knock Quinn out several times because his wolf was out of control, but the others hadn't drawn weapons before, and Jago never brought out his dragon.

Nature showed me everything like this wasn't forever etched in my memory. As the scene played in my mind, I remembered every emotion I was feeling. I felt defeated like I should have figured this out by now. I had no idea why the goblets hadn't worked. I thought I had tried everything.

My mates had enough, and even though they were driving me crazy, I didn't deserve them. They deserved someone better — someone who could pick or figure this out. Nature was playing games, and clearly, I was the target. Jago, Quinn, Colnar, and Cirrus were just pawns in some hybrid curse.

I felt the words forming in my throat. I knew they would kill me, but maybe it would release them to find their mates. I let my magic form in my finger and brought it to my throat to amplify my voice.

"I want all of you gone. I release you as being my mates. All of you." It killed me to say it, and I was looking at the floor instead of them.

What I hoped would happen would be that there would be some sort of release. Nature could keep her curse on me. I'd still feel the mate-pull, but the rest of them would finally be free. They could leave and find their true mates and not have to deal with the fucked-up consequences of being in my life.

Of course, Nature couldn't be that kind. The room erupted with all of them screaming at me. They were mad at each other for the time I spent alone with each of them instead of me. They were rightfully angry with me this time. They wanted me to fight for them. I thought I *was* fighting for them. I was giving them the chance to get away from my curse to find happiness.

I thought we were all miserable, but clearly, they all cherished their one day alone with me and wanted to keep doing it until I could figure this out. The problem was, I *couldn't* keep stringing them along, which is what it felt like I was doing. They deserved an explanation.

My tears fell freely. I'd cried about this away from them, but never in front of them,

"Please, go — all of you. I'm going to keep trying to find an answer. I'm going to fight, but I can't keep watching all of *you* fight. You're going to kill each other, and I can't deal with it. I'll keep trying, no matter how long it takes, but please, if you find someone that makes you happy, find love."

I cheated. I didn't want to hear their answer. I opened portals behind all of them and sent them back to The Order headquarters in Switzerland. I fell on the floor sobbing as soon as they disappeared. I was sobbing now as I watched the vision play out.

I felt two arms around me and knew it was Aria. It was time to contact them and apologize. I did what I promised and never stopped trying with the goblet. It just took Rainer and the entire Infinity coven to figure out what I couldn't. Aria held me until I sobbed everything out.

Nature didn't need to show me that again. That scene haunted my dreams. Every night for the past three years, it would play out, and I would wake up crying. I was done with seeing that. It was time to fix it.

I knew exactly where my mates were right now. They were at home, stinking drunk. Where I had tried to figure this out and had been haunted by what I did, my mates tried to drink their sorrows away. They were all at home right now.

I started channeling Aria as I held her hands. I'd never channeled a hybrid before. Her aura and essence were strong, unlike anything I'd channeled before. I felt a huge energy surge and reached out to my mates. I made it so everyone could hear each other. They all said my name as soon as they realized I was finally contacting them, then got pissed when they realized they weren't alone with me.

"Please, all of you. There is an answer to this. I'm not the only hybrid this happened to. I have Aria Emanuele with me, and she and her mates were able to figure out what I couldn't. Can you all come back here? Jago and Cirrus, I need you to bring herbs you can only get in dragon and Fae territory."

Jago spoke first. *"Just tell us, Liliana. I can't watch you tell me in person someone else is your mate!"*

"Jago, I have an answer that works for everyone, but there's a spell involved. I'd rather tell all of you in person instead of like this."

"Do you realize what you've done to me when you sent me away, Liliana? You know how I feed and how happy I was to meet my mate. Do you realize what you've reduced me to just knocking me into a portal like I meant nothing to you? I've existed off Hellebore and skin contact because I literally can't feed with anyone else now."

I felt guilt down to my very toes. I hated thinking about it, but I wouldn't have faulted Colnar for his nature after what I did. I felt Aria squeeze my hands. She didn't need to say a word. We weren't related in any way, but I already knew what she was trying to tell me. Neither of us had the gift of foresight, but she was here to help Colnar.

I knew from Colnar and Aria they could dream walk and soothe over dreams. Colnar *could* have visited me in my dreams and fed that way, but he must have thought he wouldn't have been welcome. The way things were left, I never tried to contact them and I just assumed because they never tried to contact me, they were furious at me. I knew now it wasn't anger. I'd hurt them deeply.

I started digging into Aria sexual energy. She wasn't my mate, so it should just look red to me. As I channeled it, I could tell hers was a beautiful light green. It didn't affect me like Colnar's violet energy, but I took it into me and let it mix with the white light that was my magic.

I felt another energy surge. I felt invincible after being with my mates for two years. I had gotten unusually strong, even if I couldn't figure the goblet out. This was a different kind of magic, and it was letting me do things both Aria and I shouldn't be able to do.

Colnar wasn't sleeping, and I couldn't normally get into people's heads unless they were in front of me. It was like I was in the same room with Colnar, but he couldn't see me. Colnar's physical body was still strong. It would be as long as he was eating properly. I knew the signs he wasn't feeding he supe side properly. I saw them in the mirror every day.

Colnar's eyes were dull like mine and sunken in from not feeding. His body was healthy, but his skin was a sickly pallor and not its usual shade of bronze. I flung out my hands and sent my light and Aria's sexual energy directly into his chest. Colnar lifted in the air and his back arched. There was almost an explosion of the violet energy I was used to seeing from him. I knocked me back to my enchanted garden and out of his bedroom.

"Liliana?" Colnar gasped. *"What did you just do? Who is*

with you? I felt someone else's sexual energy just now."

"Hello, Colnar," Aria chuckled. *"Let's keep the fact that you felt me at all to yourself. Rainer will hex your cock off."*

"So, it's true?" Cirrus said, interrupting. *"My father's ambassador was at your father's court for Unseen Moon's trial. None of the Fae know about my situation with Liliana, but news of you and your mates have reached the Fae."*

"Yes, it's true, and I'm here with Liliana. If you'll all forget what happened before and get your asses back here, Liliana has an answer and a mission for all of you. A fun one. You'll get in on the Unseen Moon action."

"What do you all say?" I asked. *"Are you ready for this mate situation to be over and get a little glory?"*

"My father's ambassador reported Unseen Moon doesn't exist anymore. How exactly are we getting any glory with the Unseen Moon situation?"

I knew that would perk my warriors up. A promise of an answer to our mate situation would have them wanting to come back. The promise of a battle would have them rushing.

I clucked my tongue. *"Everything when I can see all of your beautiful faces again."*

"Where are you now, Liliana?" Jago asked. *"And I'm guessing just hearing Colnar that you were able to somehow send him Aria's sexual energy? I'm confused. Can you open portals so we can get to you faster? I've missed you, my treasure."*

I didn't need Aria to squeeze my hands again. I didn't need her sexual energy to heal anyone again but channeling her aura, I had enough power to open portals for all of them and get them here safely without a witch there to guide them through it.

"Focus on my garden in the villa in Turkey when the portal opens. I'll be waiting."

PRESENT DAY

Aria was grinning at me when I opened my eyes as the portals started opening around us.

She stood and brushed her trousers off. "I'll have Rainer prepare the ritual table."

Before I opened the portal, I mentioned the Wineberry and Silver Jasmine to Jago and Cirrus. I was relieved to find out they both had some handy in their bedrooms and could just grab it when I opened the portal. I stayed in the safety of my stone circle. The magical hum there just made me feel safe, even though I knew I had nothing to fear from my mates.

Colnar popped through first, quickly followed by Jago, then Cirrus, then Quinn. I thought I could keep my shit together, but as soon as I saw them again, I burst into tears. I wasn't normally someone who cried a lot, and my mates had *never* seen me cry before, even with this whole mate situation. If I ever did before I sent them away, it was away from them. They only saw my tears once, the day I sent them away.

"Oh shit!" Quinn said, rushing at me as I sank to the ground.

"Liliana, are you angry with us again?" Cirrus asked, catching me before I hit the ground.

Jago kneeled in front of me and caressed my face. "My treasure, please tell me those are happy tears."

Colnar took my hand. "I'm sorry, Liliana. I was crude when you reached out. I wasn't really mad at you, and I was harsh with you. I've been hoping you'd reach out to me the past three years, and then I blew it when you finally did."

"You have no idea how much I missed all of you, even the fighting," I sobbed.

Cirrus scooped me up and started walking towards the house. "Let's get inside. It looks like it might rain. You feel like you've lost weight," Cirrus fussed. "I hope you asked for the Silver Jasmine because you want cookies."

"Liliana, have you been unable to blood feed like I was unable to feed?" Colnar asked. "Why didn't you contact us?"

I rubbed my face in Cirrus' chest. It was so nice to be back in his arms. "I thought you were all mad at me for what I did."

They all stopped when they got to the living room and saw everyone there. Cirrus pulled me closer to him, and I saw Colnar eye Aria, then her mates. He met my eye and gave me this small nod like he'd already figured out what the answer was, and he was telling me he was okay with it. Cirrus gave me this reassuring squeeze like he knew too and this was going to be okay.

It was Quinn and Jago that hadn't caught on yet, and for once, they were working together. They both stood in front of me. Jago's tongue was flickering, and Quinn was sniffing everyone. He shot Ronric this confused look.

"Ronric of the Hollow Fire pack? You keep strange company."

"Watch it, pup. It's no stranger than the company you keep. Perhaps you need to use your nose a bit more before I break it."

Thankfully, Quinn knew better than to challenge an Alpha, even if he'd picked fights with every single one of my mates. Jago was made of stone and hadn't commented, but Quinn finally just looked shocked when he realized the situation Ronric was in. Jago kept his back to me, but he finally spoke.

"I can taste how you are all her mates, and you are okay with this, but I don't understand how this is working with all of you. Lycan, you're going to have to explain how you're okay with your mate sitting in the lap of a vampire and not kill him. Because I'd like to eat the fairy right now if he doesn't put Liliana down."

Ronric was his usual crazy self and just laughed. "No eating the Fae. They are gamey buggars."

Jago finally started rumbling again as he laughed with Ronric. "Yeah, the Fae don't have a lot of fat on them to start with. Charred human, though? Just right. So, you have a solution that I don't have to get an upset stomach eating this Fae?"

If Jago was actually joking, then he wouldn't put up too much of a fight when we told him about the spell. Maybe he wouldn't argue too much about drinking the blood.

"Is someone going to explain or are we going to keep joking about the dragon's disgusting eating habits?" Quinn exploded.

"It's quite simple," I said. "Nature was correct when she kept showing me the goblet, but it took Rainer and the entire Infinity Coven to figure this out. You know I had your glyphs, and I tried your sigils. The goblet actually needed both and there needed to be a glyph for me. Rainer wrote one for hybrids. When Aria and the rest of them called to Nature, *all* of the glyphs lit up and said they were all mates. It's probably the same for us too."

"A glyph lighting up to tell us the truth isn't going to fix the fact that I don't want any of these wankers touching what's mine," Quinn growled.

Ronric gave him a knowing look. "Have you finally centered your damned wolf and figured out what you did to Liliana?"

Cirrus finally set me down, and a purple-faced Quinn turned to face me. I touched his cheek. "I know, and it's okay. Ronric explained it to me. There's an answer for all the jealousy and fighting too if you'll all just trust me."

Aria just smirked. I was starting to think that smirk was something the Incubus and Succubus did because I'd seen it on Colnar's face before.

"If you'll all just cooperate without asking questions, you're going to be in for the night of your lives."

I saw Cirrus and Colnar perk up, and I remember what Cirrus told me about Fae parties. "Night as in singular?" Cirrus looked positively intrigued like he was plotting something again.

Kalon threw back his head and laughed. "Yes, singular and you will all be fine with it."

"I don't want to see your fairy boner again," Jago growled. "You said something about Unseen Moon. If I'm finally going to get my treasure and somehow be okay with all these wankers being there, then after all this time, it needs to be a proper celebration like back in the old days. With blood, death, then sex. It's how I want to mark my mate."

Aria's smirk just grew. "I like you, Jago. We're supposed to go in as a team and wipe out the rest of Zimin's followers and destroy something called a Pith Totem. Rainer and Liliana will get the location out of the toad-man and destroy it, and we will get to have fun killing everyone in the building."

"Whose idea was this?" Cirrus demanded. "Liliana has never been put into battle before."

I punched Cirrus in the arm. "Do I need to go toe to toe with you with a battle staff and shove it up your arse to prove I can do this?"

I should have known that was going to turn Cirrus on.

"Liliana is a capable warrior," Jago said. "We've been working together with the dagger, and I've watched her with you with the staff. We both know she doesn't even need weapons with battle magic and her vampire abilities. If you ask me, it's about time Xenon let Liliana explore her warrior side."

"I agree with Jago," Quinn said. I think that was the first time Quinn had agreed with Jago on anything since we were all marked as mates. "If I get to mark Liliana after all this time and this is all somehow going to work with all of us there, I want it to be a celebration. And I think it would be sexy as hell to watch her flinging battle magic at a bunch of crazy humans intent on world domination."

"Cade left the Pith Totem in case anything happened to him. Aleksei has it, and we think Cade is trying to instruct him on how to get Cade and several others out of Tartarus," I explained.

"Then, we don't need to be thinking about sex anyway," Colnar said. "We need to be focusing on stopping Unseen Moon from getting out."

Rainer finally spoke. He had been quietly sitting at the ritual table grinding the herbs we already had.

"We should still do the spell and bind all of you, even if you don't mark Liliana yet. It will help you in battle."

"Excuse me, you intend to bind me with these cretins how?" Cirrus asked.

I sighed and turned to Cirrus. "It's the only way. It's a combination of witchcraft and a vampire blood bond. Do you see Aria and her mates? Ask them if they are happy before you start insulting my nature."

"I wouldn't—" Cirrus started.

"I was like you once," Ronric said, finally not acting totally mad. "I wasn't a total snob like a Fae, but I thought this spell was rigged. Aria's other mates are a vampire and a warlock, and we used blood and warlock magic. I was convinced the goblet was going to name Rainer as her mate because he fixed it to. When all our sigils lit up, I only briefly hesitated when this crazy warlock started drinking a goblet of blood and herbs and wanted me to do the same. As soon as I swallowed, all my hostility towards Rainer and Kalon just melted away. Now, not only did I get to mark Aria, Rainer and Kalon are like my best mates."

I was expecting an argument from all of them about drinking blood. None of them was a vampire like me. All they had was Ronric's word that he doubted and it worked. To be honest, I was expecting to get a little offended at whatever they were going to say about why they didn't want to drink the contents of the goblet because everything about the goblet except the herbs was related to my nature.

Jago looked down at me and handed me a jar. "I take it this is why you wanted the Wineberry? We should get to it because I've missed my treasure."

Cirrus came up beside me and handed me a silver bag. "I brought a lot of Silver Jasmine because I wasn't sure why you were asking. There *should* be enough in here for the spell and for me to make you Jasmine Cookies."

I'm sure my mouth was hanging open. I was expecting the most argument from Jago and Cirrus. Quinn too. Quinn just nodded at Ronric.

"I take it you've got the herbs needed for me?"

"He does, and I've got the Hellebore for Colnar," Aria said.

I walked over and handed everything to Rainer. He asked us to make a circle around his ritual table. My mates were all strong, opinionated men, but none of them made a sound as Rainer ground everything together in a stone bowl, then added it to the goblet. He started passing my athame around, and we all slashed our palms, adding our blood.

Rainer asked us to all join hands. He'd already given me the spell Infinity wrote. He and I chanted together, asking Nature for the answer. I wasn't sure exactly what happened when Rainer did this with Aria, but my glyph lit up first with a swirl of colors. It was a mix of sexual energy and the colors of the auras of all my mates.

When I was working on this alone, I had always assumed the glyph of my true mate would light up. As our chant grew louder, there was a part of me that was doubting, that I would be punished for not figuring this out on my own and none of the glyphs would light up.

I was wrong as the goblet lit up in an almost blinding swirl of colors. When our chanting stopped, so did the lights on the sigil. We all just sat there, holding hands. I had no idea who was going to drink first and if I'd have to pick an order again.

Jago scooped the goblet off the table first and held it up like he was toasting me. "To my treasure finally really being mine." He took a deep sip and passed it to the right, to Cirrus.

Cirrus held it up too and winked at me. "I've got plans for you, pet," he said, drinking.

Cirrus passed it to Quinn and Quinn didn't even hesitate. I was pretty sure it was the fact that an Alpha had done this before that had eased Quinn's mind. "I'm going to fix my mistakes, Liliana," he said, taking a deep drink.

Colnar's smirk was back when he took the goblet. "I've missed you so much, beloved."

He drained the goblet and slammed it down on the table. No one said anything. They just all eyed each other, and I was starting to wonder if it didn't work the same for me as it did with Aria. Maybe we should have altered the spell?

Finally, Jago's dragon started rumbling again as he laughed. "Oh, Liliana. I don't want to eat any of them anymore, and you've never been to a dragon celebration after a battle. And a dragon celebration where I'll be marking you. I'm already planning it, and you're going to have a *hell* of a night."

"I've got some ideas too," Cirrus said.

Quinn grinned. "What do you say, Jago? As shifters, we should mark her together."

"You read my mind, Lycan."

Jago was right. I didn't think I'd be able to handle

whatever they were planning now that they didn't want to kill each other. They were all warriors, and I already knew what we would be doing was going to be extra intense because they were celebrating battle.

I was more nervous about what was going to happen when they all marked me than trying to destroy a Pith Totem and going on my first mission they were actually letting me fight.

PRESENT DAY

I was shocked at the change in my mates as we planned our battle. It was like the last five years never happened and they had been lifelong best friends. Jago and Quinn were starting a tally sheet of how many men their beasts could bring down and were turning it into a bit of a contest. If I didn't know better, Cirrus was flirting with Colnar a little stroking his ego about how many warriors he could take down. Colnar was flirting right back and saying Cirrus was no slouch himself when it came to fighting.

If I wasn't sitting there with Aria and her mates watching them do the exact same thing, minus the flirting, I would have thought I was in some alternate reality. Ronric and Kalon had started their own tally about how many people they were going to kill, and it seemed like Aria was getting turned on about getting to fight with Ronric.

She jumped in his lap and kissed him. "Unlike The Battle of Clontarf and that pub of mercenaries, we'll finally get to celebrate a victory like the old days."

"Not quite like the old days," Ronric said, nipping at her nose. "Only the Fae celebrate like we do."

Cirrus overheard that. "This Fae is coming up with an elaborate plot on how he wants to celebrate."

"How have I never been invited to a Fae party before?" Aria laughed.

Cirrus grinned. "Because your dear old Papa would boil us in hot oil."

Aria just shrugged. "Maybe when I was younger. He seems to be okay with my mate situation."

I changed the subject back to the battle ahead of us. I was still nervous about the whole marking thing. Xenon had given us the coordinates in Russia. Aleksei had moved from an apartment to a secluded villa, much like Zimin had. The vampire woman who was getting intel from Aleksei had gotten banned from the compound.

We were pretty sure it was the Pith Totem. Aleksei had it out while she was with him. Cade would have noticed a vampire and wasn't taking any chances. Vampire compulsion eventually wore off. *My* compulsion as a hybrid didn't. That was why The Order wanted me so badly. We were all pretty sure Cade told Aleksei to lock himself in his bedroom and talked him through it through the Pith Totem.

She'd given The Order the coordinates for the villa and a good idea of where Aleksei's bedroom was for portals. I'd been benched for the whole Zimin thing, but I'd heard about his villa. Zimin's villa had high walls, armed guards, and security camera, but from what Aria told me, it was like one big party inside.

Our intel on Aleksei's villa was that he was there because of the upped security. Steel doors, panic rooms, and way more armed guards. It was going to be a bloodbath, and that seemed to be what everyone was craving. Rainer could only open portals and send people through them if he was with them. I could open them and have them end up where they needed to go without needing to be holding onto anyone.

The plan was for me to open two portals. One would get everyone by the pool area, which was reported not to be heavily guarded. They would spill into the house killing anything that moved. The second portal would be for Rainer and me and would get us as close to Aleksei's room as possible. Between the two of us, our magic could blast through steel doors.

Rainer put his hand over mine. "How much experience do you have with Pith Totems?"

"Not up close. It was outlawed before I was born."

"Same here. Has The Order trained you?"

"Yes, I've had training. We're going to have to channel each other, and it's going to fight back. From what I understand, the Pith Totem can't attack us, but Cade's pith is going to fight to stay. It's going to try to trick us."

"That's about what I know too. Does battle magic kill it?"

"Yes, but I think we should actually let him talk first. We can find out if there are any more totems and maybe he'll spill his plans."

"Yes, Voldemort made seven Horcruxes," Kalon said, nodding like I was supposed to understand that. "Why are you staring at me again? When we get back, and after all the marking is done, I'm going to force all of you to watch Harry Potter so you can see what you're missing."

"Kalon," Rainer warned. "We needed to be focusing on Pith Totems, not human fiction. What do you mean by trick us, Liliana? Pith Totems were outlawed before I was born, so I only know theories."

Something I knew and Rainer didn't? That was a first. "Eventually, all of you will have to go to Switzerland for specialized training with The Order. There's probably not much they can teach all of you about fighting, but they train witches and warlocks on forbidden spells and how to break them. There's also tomes about all our natures, and they might teach you something new about how to use it in battle."

Thankfully, no one brought up The Order didn't teach me anything about figuring out my mate situation. They were all working on it just as hard as I was. We knew a lot of things, but we couldn't figure that out.

"I look forward to the training. But let's focus on the now and that Pith Totem."

I nodded. "Cade's pith was split, and part of it placed into the totem, so it has magic. Cade can see everything through the totem and communicate through it, but he'll be limited in his magic since his physical form is in the Underworld. This is the first Pith Totem I've come across, but there are several spells he could cast. He can't move the totem where we can't find it, but he can make damned sure we don't want to be in the same room with it."

"Can he cast forbidden curses from the totem?" Rainer asked, starting to look uncomfortable.

"Yes, but unless he's met someone in the Underworld to teach them to him, I don't think Unseen Moon knows them, or they would have done them by now. He'll try compulsion and illusions — things he knows. He can't make the same magic bomb he used on us before from a Pith Totem. I can't be compelled, and I can put a blessing on you so you can't be either while we're in there. It will eventually wear off. "

"Do the blessing," Cirrus said. "She does it for us and refreshes it all the time. That's why she wasn't able to compel our asses to behave during our situation."

Aria snorted. "She should have. If I could do it like she can, I would have if I had thought of it."

"Do you think Cade found someone in the Underworld to teach him those spells?" Quinn asked. He also looked worried.

"I doubt it," Jago said. Out of everyone here, Jago was the oldest and would know the most about The Underworld. "You sent them there while they were alive, right? The other beings there would be hunting them down. They would think if they found a way *in,* then they would know a way *out.* And compulsion doesn't work on piths in the Underworld. No supernatural gift works down there. The piths would be wanting to take control of Unseen Moon's bodies hoping they could just walk right out of the Underworld."

I'd never met Cade. I'd never met anyone in Unseen Moon. My missions had never involved the long-standing investigation into Unseen Moon until they finally showed their true colors and I realized I'd been cleaning up their dirty politicians for centuries. Just dealing with the dirty humans that chose to follow him, somehow, I thought Cade's experience in the Underworld was going to be different than what Jago thought. He'd convinced countless humans to overthrow governments and start wars.

"Would a pith in the Underworld stop long enough to listen if Cade offered them a deal?" I asked. "We know Cade planned on getting out. What if he promised piths a way out and a body if he escapes?"

"Well, that's never going to happen," Rainer scoffed. "There's no way out of the Underworld. No spell can bring anyone back and believe me, people have tried writing them. Can you imagine how many bereaved witches and warlocks have tried to write spells to bring loved ones back? It's never been accomplished in our entire history. That doesn't mean witches and piths keep hoping someone will find that spell. Cade could very well have been taught a forbidden hex since The Order already destroyed one of his totems and he knows they are onto him."

I just grinned at him. Rainer was starting to pace, worried about getting hit by a forbidden hex. "I'm more worried about any illusions he may cast. By the time I was invited to The Order, they'd already figured out how to defend against those curses. Cade will resort to compulsion when he realizes his curses aren't working, then illusion when he knows that doesn't work either.

"The problem is going to be locating the totem and destroying it before he creates some horrible illusion. The totem can be anything. Cade could very well have used a simple ink pen to hide in plain sight."

"No, that's not Cade," Aria said, shaking her head. "At least, not the Cade I met when I was sixteen. Cade is arrogant and spoiled. He likes to show off. It wouldn't shock me if his totem is one of the gods humans worship, something they hold sacred. That totem could very well be an old Orthodox human crucifix since he concentrated on Russia," Aria said. "He pretty much held nothing for our people sacred, and he probably blasphemes the humans too."

"I agree," Rainer said. Kalon nodded too and finally hadn't brought those movies up again. They'd all met

Cade, and I hadn't. "If Cade wanted to convince someone to overthrow governments and start wars, what better way than to pretend like he's a god?"

"Cade's a real turd. I wish your dad had let us knock him around a bit. Only a wanker like Cade would still be causing trouble from fucking Tartarus," Ronric growled.

"Well, Liliana seems to know how to protect Rainer and together, they can destroy the Pith Totem. Rainer and Liliana are both capable warriors and can handle any goons that are sure to be outside the toad man's door. When do we do this?"

Quinn finally stood and came to stand next to me. "I know I'm young compared to the rest of you. I'm a trained warrior too and can handle myself. Liliana and Rainer have a difficult battle, but this will probably be easy for the rest of us. That said, my Alpha always taught us this—something can always go wrong, and you never go into battle with things left unsaid. I think we all have things we need to say to Liliana before this happens."

All my mates were nodding. Ronric came over and put Quinn in a playful headlock. "So, the pup really *is* a grown Lycan. I like you, Quinn, and I'd be honored to rip out some throats with you. Go talk this out."

I gulped as my mates filed out to my bedroom. I knew what was coming. They needed to hash out how mad they were at me, so they weren't distracted in battle. They needed to say it in case something happened and it never got said.

I needed to hear it because this was all my fault.

PRESENT DAY

To say I was shocked when all four of my mates hopped in my bed and seemed to want me to join them instead of yell at me would be an understatement.

"Treasure, let us hold you for what needs to be said. You have this tension in your shoulders like you are carrying this burden yourself. You're too much of a good person to blame us for what happened too, but we are more at fault than you think you are for this."

"Come here, pet," Cirrus said, patting the bed. "My Illumination has other uses too. Let me help you get rid of some of that tension."

I hesitated. I watched them all drink from the goblet, and I heard their words. I could see them all lounging on the bed together like they were friends again. But I watched them fight for so long, and there was a part of me that thought Nature was playing tricks. This wouldn't work for me the way it worked for Aria.

They all noticed. Quinn sprung from the bed, and

before I knew it, he had me in his arms, and I was gently placed in the bed next to Cirrus. Quinn shot me this adoring look, and it didn't look like he was going to rip Cirrus' throat out.

"Liliana, you look tense and ill-fed. Please, let Cirrus help, then you need to feed properly," Quinn said. "And Jago is right. I didn't call us in here to yell at you. I think we all want to apologize to you."

"Apologize to *me?* I was the one that shoved you all in portals and sent you away!" I was prepared for an argument. I *wanted* them to yell at me. We needed to air this out before I went up against armed guards and a Pith Totem.

"I thought *I* was the one who liked being punished," Cirrus said, grabbing my waist and hauling me up so that I was sitting between his legs. I felt his hands on my shoulders, and his Illumination felt different this time. It wasn't sexual. It was like a huge hug and the best massage of my life all at once. I almost forgot I needed to be hearing this.

"Liliana, you've been beating yourself up all this time instead of blaming us too," Cirrus said, sending his Illumination into my knotted shoulders as he gave me a massage. "It never should have been up to just you to figure this out. If I had been thinking straight instead of the overwhelming desire to mark you as my mate and kill the others, *I* should have been helping you with the spell. Fae have magic too, even if it's different from yours. I should have been with you helping you figure out that goblet instead of causing drama. It's unbecoming of a Fae prince."

"We all should have been helping you instead of starting fights and demanding all of your time when we were alone with you," Jago said. He was holding my hand and stroking the top with his thumb. "I can't write spells, and I don't have magic like Cirrus, but if you needed Wineberry, *I* should have figured that out."

"I should have centered my wolf before I ever set foot in our house again. Every baby Lycan is taught this. After an injury like what we had, that should have been my priority. The entire time everything was going on with us, I never centered him. I knew I was out of control and fighting with him, but I couldn't bear to be away from you long enough to do it. When you were with the others, I could feel it, and it set me into a rage. I should have gone running then, and I was too stupid to do the obvious.

"It was like this switch went off inside me when the mate-pull started where everything I knew and all my common sense went out the window. The only thing I *did* know was that I needed to mark you as soon as I could. If I could do that, then the others would go away. That was my wolf talking. I did some things there are no ways to apologize for. I promised I wouldn't claim you and I did anyway. I didn't realize until you sent us away and I finally did center my wolf. I was too ashamed and guilty to try to contact you and admit what I did, and I thought I had ruined everything when you sent us away."

"I think we all realized what we did to you after enough time apart," Colnar said, twirling a piece of my long black hair around his finger. "I knew for sure when I saw you again looking like you weren't able to feed like I was. You healed me when you found out, and you *still* haven't asked for our blood. You put our situation above your own needs again.

"Did you ever stop to think you may have found the

answer yourself if it wasn't for our constant demands and fighting? I believed you when you said you'd never stop trying before you sent us through the portals. I knew that was the real reason you went out of contact. No matter how miserable I got without feeding properly, I never tried to contact you. I knew if I did, I'd be distracting you from finding the answer and you'd try to help me."

"None of us were mad at you about the portals, treasure. I know that's why you think you are in here. When we ended up in Switzerland, we got into this huge brawl, blaming each other for you sending us away," Jago explained. "Most of The Order came spilling out, and several warriors had to get involved to pull us apart. It was the witches and warlocks that ended up having to knock us out that ended the fight. There was a tribunal."

My mouth hung up. Tribunals were for crimes, not mate situation. Certainly not a brawl between a few Order members. I'd seen those at headquarters. Order members sleeping with each other, relationship drama, sometimes clan feuds trickled in. It got sorted, but there was never a tribunal.

"Did they kick you out? Is that why you were with your people instead of at headquarters? Why did Xenon want you on this mission if you're not in The Order anymore?"

The knots in my back were gone, and Cirrus was now using his Illumination to play with my hair. I had to try really hard to concentrate and not just curl up on the bed and purr like a cat or Jago's dragon.

Colnar just chuckled, and his familiar smirk was back. "It wasn't like a trial where they were passing sentence. It was more like they all put us to questioning, then took their turns telling us we were all a bunch of stupid wankers. Velorina was there."

"Velorina?" I whispered in awe. She was Piero's sister and founded The Order of The Red Shadow with him. She was the High Inquisitor now, but she only got involved with major cases. She would have been involved with Unseen Moon. I was told Velorina wanted me for The Order, but I'd never met her.

Quinn flopped at the foot of the bed and started rubbing my feet. His long hair fell in his eyes. It seemed like he thought it was totally normal for us to be all in bed like this. "Velorina is even scarier than you are when she's angry, except unlike our statuesque goddess, she's maybe five feet tall tops. When she starts yelling, she's bigger than Ronric or Jago. I nearly ran away with my tail between my legs."

I wanted to push that lock of hair out from in front of his eyes so badly, but I heard Jago's dragon rumble as he chuckled. "Velorina is quite fond of you, treasure. After eating our heads off and telling us what fools we've been, she yelled at the rest of the room and told them to fix our issue too. She wanted to know why it hadn't been done yet. She didn't blame you either. She saw what you apparently couldn't. We were distracting you, and the entire Order should have figured something out by the time things got to the point they did. No one was mad at you, Liliana. Everyone was mad at The Order or us."

"We were all given orders to go home and only contact you if you contacted us first," Cirrus said, running his fingers through my hair. I swear between Cirrus' fingers in my hair and Quinn massaging my feet, I was about to pass out from pleasure. "We were told we shamed our clans. Velorina told us not to shame ourselves further and talk about this outside The Order. Everyone was ordered to leave you in peace until someone had the answer, but that wasn't the right thing to do, was it?"

"You don't have to say it out loud, Liliana, but we know now that we've drunk from that goblet," Jago said. "You don't need to be coddled, and you aren't a child, but isolation wasn't what you needed, and you could have used a few kind words or words of encouragement. Clearly, we didn't give that to you, but Velorina or Xenon could have. If Xenon showed his face here and only gave orders looking at you like that, we're all going to punch his smug face in."

I had no idea if telling them this was going to have them wanting to attack Xenon even more. I had no idea if all that rage they held towards each other was going to get directed toward Xenon if I let this slip, but they needed to know. Xenon was just under Velorina in rank. If she had gotten involved in my situation and they attacked Xenon, she'd give them all the final death.

"Xenon portalled in with orders and he was the only one who could get me to feed. Xenon had to force his blood down my throat more than once."

They didn't get angry at all. They all wanted me to bite them, and I was worried the fighting was going to start again over the order I bit them in. Clearly, I was wrong. Colnar wanted to play director.

"You're closest to Cirrus, so bite him first. I'm worried about you, Liliana because I went through what you did. Jago is right next to you, so bite him next. If Quinn can get his hands off your feet, he can go next. I want to go last so I can tell you my story. It's similar to yours."

I knew no one was upset with me, not even The Order. But I needed to hear Colnar's story so that I could finally forgive myself.

PRESENT DAY

I was transported back to three years ago as Colnar told me his story. His story paralleled mine, but I didn't dare go anywhere near my family. My mother wasn't as understanding as Colnar's apparently was. I bit my mates to feed, but I wasn't enjoying their blood like I normally did or how much I should have been having to put off blood feeding for so long because I was listening intently to Colnar.

I got a little more backstory after Velorina screamed at my mates and everyone in The Order. I'd been trained by some Order members on the council. The warlock who taught me how to guide people through portals without being present pulled the same trick I did with my mates. Almost as soon as Velorina ate their head off, Colnar told me they were sucked into portals and sent home like I had sent them to The Order. It had to be Callum because he was the one that taught me how to do that.

Colnar didn't want to feed with anyone else. He thought it was cheating. He was trying to exist off Hellebore and food. Colnar wasn't royalty like Cirrus or Aria and her mates. Colnar came from a long line of warriors, and they lived comfortably now. Most of his family was happy to retire from the fighting except Colnar.

Much like I couldn't hide putting off feeding from my mother, Colnar's family knew the signs too. They knew exactly what it meant too. Well, they knew exactly three reasons for it. Colnar had either found his mate, and they weren't of their kind. Colnar's mate needed time to come to terms with an Incubus as their mate. The other theory would be he had fallen under the thrall of another Incubus or Succubus and just needed to be kept away from them until it wore off. The last reason that would keep an Incubus or Succubus from feeding would be they angered a witch or warlock and had been hexed.

Colnar refused to speak, and his parents weren't like mine. They would wait until Colnar was ready to talk instead of screaming like my mother would have done. They were warriors, like my mother, but much more mellow because they didn't have a vampire's temper. My mother would have done what Xenon had done several times. Held me down and forced blood down my throat.

Xenon's blood used to taste wonderful to me, but after I met my mates, it kept me from totally drying out, but it was tasteless. It was like living off water. Every time his bland blood hit my throat, it would just rip off old wounds when I remembered the distinct tastes of my mates' blood that first time I bit them after I woke up after the magic bomb and how I foolishly believed everything would work out.

Colnar's parents obviously loved him, and since his nature was different, the solution was a little gentler. I had to have blood, fresh from the vein. I could put it off a little longer because of my witch side, but I'd still get to a point I'd dry out without it.

Colnar could feed by skin contact. It wasn't like sex and wouldn't keep him as strong as if he was feeding that way, but between the Hellebore and the skin contact, it would keep him from dying. I had just stupidly assumed he'd take lovers when I sent him away and I couldn't fault him for it. I should have known if I couldn't drink anyone else's blood, he'd find himself in the same situation I was in.

His parents were patient. They provided him with all the Hellebore he needed. They weren't royalty, but they did have status and a dungeon full of those that misbehaved. I'm pretty sure only in Incubus territory were criminals punished by long cuddle sessions with an Incubus warrior.

I'd long finished biting Cirrus, Jago, and Quinn. I hadn't bit Colnar because he was still telling me his story. That familiar smirk came back.

"You know, I knew exactly what the vampire was talking about when he mentioned Harry Potter?"

I moaned. "Please tell me you didn't watch that vampire movie he told us about."

"One of the Succubae my father sent to me, she was in the dungeon because she fell in love with a human. We can't mate with humans. She was in love with him as a human and loved several human things. She knew what she did was wrong, she was just glad she wasn't getting the final death for it. She was happy just to lie there pressing herself against my back for hours, but she did ask that I acquire subscriptions to several human television and movie services. Netflix is actually pretty handy. I'm going to keep my account."

"So, you snuggled and watched human television?" I asked.

I couldn't judge him for that. When we had time, we all liked some human television. I liked human crime drama, Quinn liked some sort of genre where walking dead people ate brains, and Jago liked secret agent shows. We weren't totally ignorant about human entertainment, but Colnar seemed to like stage entertainment the best.

Colnar's smirk broke into a goofy grin. He pulled me into his lap and wrapped his arms around my waist. I sighed when I felt the familiar hum of his sexual energy. I missed this.

"That movie Kalon mentioned is actually really good. The witchy one, not the vampire one. But we are going to keep you quite occupied after we mark you."

I gulped. They all wanted just to sleep tonight and it was nice being held by all of them while we slept, but I was still thinking about what was going to happen when they marked me. Could I handle it?

PRESENT DAY

We were all refreshed when we woke up early the next morning. Apparently, Cirrus had gotten out of bed and portalled somewhere to get me battle clothes. He handed me a garment bag for when I went to the shower. I just grinned after my shower when I unzipped the bag and pulled the garment out the bag. He bought me battle leathers. Finely made Fae battle leathers at that.

I pulled the supple brown leather over my slim hips. The trousers fit perfectly. The vest was a greenish leather that matched my eyes perfectly. I laced up the front ready to kick some ass. When I opened the door and came out, they were all dressed in their leathers too, and they all groaned when they saw me.

Jago adjusted his erection. "I'm keeping you in bed for days when we get back. But we have a battle to fight first."

I was strutting out to the kitchen like the ultimate badass. I lost any cred I might have had when I saw

Kalon in the kitchen and smelled frying bread and heard the sizzle of oil.

I squealed like a child. "Mekitsi?" I was hoping it was.

Kalon looked up from the skillet with a grin. "And Popara for the Lycan who still eats like a child."

My mouth was watering. "Make enough for Quinn and me too, yeah?"

Ronric seemed to have forgotten ever being angry with Quinn for how he claimed me. He stalked over to him and put him in a huge headlock. Ronric dragged Quinn all the way over to the breakfast bar.

"I ate all your cereal. You're going to have to tell me who is sending you all that beautiful Kaptain Kookie stuff."

I couldn't seem to stop smiling. They hadn't marked me, and after I'd fed and finally gotten a good night's sleep, I was less worried about it. Quinn and Ronric were playing, Kalon was cooking my favorite Bulgarian break-fast, and I was dressed like a badass. The only thing left was to destroy Cade's Pith Totem and be with my mates.

Aria was dressed similar to me, but her leathers were black. She had her long red hair down and flowing down her back like a crimson river. I had pinned mine up in a bun. Aria walked over to me and started pulling pins out my hair. I shook it out, and my long, black hair tickled my bare arms. Aria told me to wait there and came bounding back in the room with boots with a six-inch heel. The heel was sturdy, but I didn't think I could fight in it.

I was six feet tall in my bare feet. Aria was only maybe two inches shorter than me, but in her heeled boots, she was taller than me now. When I first started dealing with politicians, women didn't wear heels. I was less aggressive then and tried to gain their favor before I compelled them. They wouldn't have liked a tall woman.

Now, I went in brute force, compelling anyone in my way. I *wanted* to wear those boots, just not to my first fight. Aria saw my hesitation.

"Look. Click the heels together, and a knife pops out the front and the back. They are also enchanted, so the heel never breaks and you won't turn your ankle. It's up to you, but the boots are a weapon too. We're about the same size."

I grinned and started pulling the boots on. I zipped them up and stood. Colnar was right next to me as soon as I stood. I was almost his height now. He grabbed me and pulled me to his chest.

"Can you keep those on later?" he growled.

Aria just laughed. "Keep them. Every girl needs a pair of fuck me battle boots. I have several, and I'll give you the name of the Coven who makes them. Let's eat and kill things."

Eating breakfast with my mates and Aria's just seemed like the most natural thing to be doing. It felt like the last five years had never happened. I felt happy, satisfied, and my mates hadn't even marked me yet. This could only get better.

I watched them with small smiles, not remembering all the bad memories, as my mates joked with Aria's mates. Colnar and Aria were comparing stories, Jago and Rainer were engrossed in talking about magic, Quinn and Ronric were fast friends, and I don't know if I was shocked or not Cirrus had buddied up with Kalon. When I listened in, Cirrus was trying to find out if Kalon knew anything about why he got so aroused when I bit him.

The breakfast bar had so many conversations going

on at once. There were sex stories, magical conversations, erotic theories about vampire bites. I didn't get involved in any of them. I was content just to sit back and soak in the peace of everyone getting along.

I wasn't even thinking about the battle to come. I'd practically inhaled my food and was just watching everyone bond over breakfast. Aria slammed her coffee mug down and startled me out of my reverie.

"Let's go kick some ass!" Aria yelled.

Quinn and Ronric both threw back their heads and howled. Jago's dragon rumbled so loudly the plates were clattering on the counter. Rainer's eyes flashed gold and Colnar's flashed violet. Rainer's eye widened, but stayed the color of a gold coin.

"Your eyes are quite startling. And it's unusual you, and your mates are reacting to Aria's battle cry too."

"We can figure that out when we get back," I said.

My body reacted immediately and almost involuntarily to Aria's words. My eyes would have glowed just like Rainer's because of both my vampire blood and my magic roared to life as soon as Aria let out a modern-day battle cry. Five hundred years ago, it would have been longer, and the words would have been much more flowery, but today, kicking ass would do.

I decided to see if it would work for me. A flagon of mead was standard, but I raised my coffee cup. "To the enchanted garden!" I yelled.

Quinn and Ronric started howling again. Jago's dragon rumbled even louder. Aria, Rainer, and Colnar started hooting. We made our way to my garden. It would be early in Russia, and hopefully, everyone would still be sleeping except a few guards.

I waved my hands and opened two portals with the

coordinates given to me. One would bring Rainer and me hopefully, close to Aleksei's bedroom and the other would bring Aria and the others to the pool area. I watched my mates disappear into one portal. I wasn't all that worried for them. I was sure they could handle themselves against any human. There would be no magic bombs waiting for us this time as far as I knew.

Rainer and I stepped through the second portal. What was waiting for us concerning human guards and what Cade had learned in the Underworld was unknown.

I wasn't scared. I could do this.

PRESENT DAY

The vampire who gave Xenon the coordinates for me and Rainer's portal must have had free reign of this compound or compelled the shit out of everyone here. Rainer and I came through the portal and ended up on top of each other in some sort of closet. It had to be a hall closet because it was tiny and we were smashed together. The heel of those boots Aria gave me was standing right on his foot.

"Shit, sorry," I whispered, trying to find another place to put my foot.

"It's okay. Listen for heartbeats so we can get out of here and get the Pith Totem."

I reached out with all my senses. I wasn't just listening for heartbeats. I was trying to sense the magic of that Pith Totem. It didn't take long. It usually didn't, and we weren't out of range for my gifts to work. Rainer and I may have been fucked. The vampire who gave these coordinates couldn't have picked a closet inside Aleksei's bedroom or further down the hall?

"We're right across the hall from the room with the

Pith Totem. There are six heartbeats outside this door. I think there's four guarding the door and two inside. The four heartbeats outside the door are quickened like they've taken something. The two inside are racing because I think they are having sex. If Jago were here, he could tell us what kind of weapons they have," I whispered.

"That feeling of wrongness about fifteen feet away, is that the totem? Can it sense us and warn anyone?"

"Yes, that creepy feeling you're getting is the totem. From what I've been taught, it can sense danger, which means when we open this door and start fighting the guards, the totem will sense magic is being done outside the room. If Cade has learned any forbidden curses in the Underworld, he'll start chanting to cast them."

"And we'll have trouble getting in there because Xenon said it's built like a safe room. Aleksei presses a button, and a steel door slides down."

"A magic blast would blow through the door, kill the guard, and disrupt the totem," I suggested.

"It could also bring the entire house down."

I listened again, honing in on the heartbeats: four men, four hands between us. Two were straddling the door, and two were against the wall. Rainer and I were so close, we could talk without being overheard and didn't need to talk telepathically. That would have tipped Cade's Pith Totem off if he was listening.

"How strong is your battle magic and how good is your aim?" I asked.

"I think I know where you are going with this. If you point me in the right direction, we can take out the guards and the door before it becomes a fully functional safe room."

"Don't go straight in the bedroom," I warned. "Stay in the hall until we are sure what Cade's defenses are. I don't think I know everything Pith Totems are capable of because no one ever thought I'd go up against one. Hold your hands about thirty-five centimeters apart and blast with everything you have."

Rainer squeezed my hand. "On three?"

Rainer held his hands out, but before he could count, I adjusted them a little to aim better at the heartbeats I was hearing. I thrust my own hands out and waited for the countdown. On three, our tiny closet lit up with the blinding white light of battle magic, and the door and wall in front of us exploded. By the time the dust cleared, the wall across the hall was also reduced to dust. In a perfect world, we would have taken Aleksei and the Pith Totem out too.

Rainer looked like he was going to go charging into the bedroom, but I stopped him. Aleksei, the toad-man was sitting up in bed, as if in a trance. The woman he was having sex with had a ritual athame stuck in her chest. Aleksei was painting symbols in the old tongue on his chest with her blood.

Aleksei was human and shouldn't have known a word of the old tongue or those glyphs. I could also tell whatever spell he was casting was almost done and Rainer and I would be stupid to enter that room until we knew what that spell was and how Aleksei knew it. *I* didn't know it, and as far as I knew, I had been trained on all the forbidden curses.

I whispered to Rainer telepathically to let him complete the spell because if I could hear the majority of it, I could figure out how to undo it. I'd missed the beginning of it. I'd just hoped I'd heard enough to write a counterspell.

Aleksei stood up, the sheet falling from his naked body. His torso and face were covered with the blood glyphs he had painted on sloppily. His eyes glowed a dull shade of gray, almost like tarnished silver. He started sniffing the air.

When he spoke, his accent wasn't Russian like it was supposed to be. He didn't speak in Russian at all. "Ah, the wife stealer and curser of witches. And...a little baby witch hybrid? My first hybrid was a dud, but I could use you, especially with your witch blood."

Cade. He'd somehow transferred his pith from the Pith Totem to Aleksei. No one told me this was possible and I had no idea how much power Cade had in Aleksei's body with just part of his pith. I also didn't know if he'd learned something we didn't want in the Underworld. Hell, I didn't know if he learned *this* spell in The Underworld.

I heard Rainer in my head. *"He loves to talk. Aria told us about her showdown with him. He was able to immobilize her totally, but if he hasn't done that yet, he's not at full power. I didn't get enough of his spell to try to reverse it."*

"I don't think I did either. I don't think Cade is dumb enough to repeat his mistakes and talk a second time."

"That's why you have to trick him. Cade has wanted a hybrid for a very long time. He thinks hybrids are the answer to all his problems. Use that and get intel. He's not casting anything forbidden yet. I don't think he's strong enough."

I let my eyes go to slits and took a step away from Rainer. I'd learned a few lessons from Colnar over the years. I knew from Aria Cade wanted to make a witch hybrid with her, and here I was standing in front of him.

He'd lost his mate and his queen with all his trickery. I could use that. And Cade had no idea who he was dealing with.

My special brand of compulsion was subtle. Not even a supe knew I was doing it, especially since I could do it from across the room and my eyes didn't betray me by glowing. I started weaving a small web of compulsion and sent it towards Cade.

"You must be a very strong warlock to be speaking to me from the body of a human when you're supposed to be in the Underworld," I purred. "Much stronger than the warlock I'm with." I looked back at Rainer. Let Cade think we were together. He would have no way of knowing how the hybrid mate situation worked in the end.

Cade threw back his head and laughed. "So, the Succubus slut didn't want you either? Tell me, did she pick the vampire I tortured since he's more like her? Do you think you even cross her mind when she's biting and fucking him? Has the mate-pull gone away?"

I was hoping the mate-pull didn't ruin this for us. I hoped Rainer didn't just react and kill Cade in this body before I got what I needed because he was saying awful things about Aria. I didn't turn around. I just braced myself and prepared to react for whatever happened next.

"Aria is not the only hybrid. As you can see, I found another one."

"And based on how she's looking at me in his ugly man's body, you've lost this one too. When I'm back on this planet, I'll make her my queen, restore what you took from us, and wipe you all out."

I was starting to wonder how Cade stayed hidden for

so long. Talking to him now, he was pretty stupid. He was making the exact same mistake he made when he got caught the first time. My compulsion had something to do with that, but I was practically playing him like a violin.

"I'm sure your true form is much more pleasant on the eyes than this one," I said, laying on the flattery. "How do you intend to get out of the Underworld so I can truly be your queen?" I said, taking another step forward. "How are you in the ugly man now?"

"Old magic taught to me by a witch in the Underworld. It was just a theory, but I see it's possible. If I had known it was you, I would have kept my Pith Totem intact. Once I was able to ensure my safety in the Underworld and make a connection with my totem, the witch taught me a chant. It allowed more of my pith to enter the totem. My body in the Underworld is slowly dying as my pith goes into the totem. Once enough of it was in the totem, I would have had Aleksei bring me warriors. I would have had my choice of a new body."

"How will you do it now that your Pith Totem is destroyed, my king?" I asked.

"Well, my beautiful little hybrid, we're going to kill the warlock who stole my wife and cursed my coven and four other covens. I take it you can dispatch whoever is making all that racket outside. Then we regroup. I have a safe house hidden in Unseen Moon territory in a mountain. Raffaele's men wouldn't have found it. You'll portal us there. There are all sorts of forbidden things in my safe house. You'll kill this body and make me a new Pith Totem. Since you'll be my queen, I'll let you pick the body you're attracted to."

Cade gave me the creeps, even if he wasn't in the

body of a man who looked like a toad and I didn't know all his crimes. He thought it was that easy to win a woman over. Just a little show of power in an ugly body and I was his. No wonder Aria spent centuries running from him before we all knew Unseen Moon was evil.

"My king, it sounds like there are dangerous elements outside these walls. Let me portal you to your safe house, kill your enemies, and then we can start this process to put you in a body I desire."

The wide, toad looking face finally looked suspicious. I was wondering when he'd finally doubted me. He couldn't be totally stupid if he managed to stay hidden for so long and had figured out how to get out of the Underworld. I was worried he'd ask me to hurt Rainer before he gave up the location of his safe house. So far, he'd just seemed to have ignored him or thought of him as some pest I could easily take care of for him.

It just hit me Cade was telling me all of his secrets and wanted me for his queen, and the bastard hadn't even bothered finding out my name yet. He had enough magic to feel I was a hybrid and that was all that mattered to him. I wonder if he made Aria feel the same way when she met him and that was the only reason she spent so many years running. It was like Cade didn't care who we were as women or what we might want. Our dual nature was all he cared about.

Just then, Quinn and Ronric both let out howls. I knew Quinn's howls by now. I knew when his wolf howled from pleasure, from pain, or because he'd spotted his prey on a hunt. That howl was because Quinn was having fun fighting alongside another Lycan and finally being put back into battle. It had the effect I hoped it did.

"Lycans are here?" Cade asked in a panic. Clearly, he wasn't strong enough to knock anyone out or conjure a Hellfire Cage, or he would have done so by now. Cade was vulnerable like this, and it was his last chance at escaping the Underworld. His Pith Totem was destroyed. If he died in Aleksei's body, there was no coming back for him. But I needed the location of that safe house because he said there were forbidden things there and that could mean his father or other Unseen Moon members had Pith Totems stashed there.

"Quick, my king. The Lycans here are savage and will rip your throat out. The location of your safe house. I'll kill them once I know you are safe."

"Not in front of the warlock. He'll commune with the other covens and tell them. Kill him, then I'll tell you."

Damn. I was hoping we wouldn't get to this point. Aria was going to be pissed, and I had no desire to hurt Rainer. I needed a plan. I could cast without chanting, and I didn't think Cade had enough magic to sense what I was doing.

"Rainer, I'm going to put a sleeping spell on you. Try to act like it hurts."

What I really did was send healing light at Rainer that would have just felt like a tickle and enchanted him to fall asleep on the spot. The healing light would look enough like battle magic to fool someone not familiar with it, but I didn't know if it was enough to fool Cade. He was smart enough to weasel a solution out of a witch in the Underworld, but pretty stupid to trust my lies.

"Quick, my queen before the Lycans come. You need to get me to safety at the highest point of the Danube Hills."

"Rainer is a tricky warlock. Let me make sure he's actually dead."

So far, Cade hadn't used the same trick on us he'd used on Aria. I didn't think he was capable of it, but if he was, I didn't have her Succubus abilities to get out of it like she did. I was going to have to use my fight training to kill him. He still believed I was going to portal him to the Danube Hills to safety, be his queen, and help him commit mass murder again.

"Be quick with it," he snapped, tapping his toe. "You'll learn when you're my queen not to make me wait for things, and you'll learn your place."

Oh, *no one* talked to me like that. I was looking forward to killing Cade a second time. I crouched down and pretended to check Rainer with my magic for signs of life. What I was actually doing was pulling an ornate dagger Jago gave me and trained me with from my boot.

Cade hardly got a chance to complain more when I used my vampire speed to speed into a roll and fling my dagger at him. My aim was true, and Cade found my dagger buried in his chest. He looked so confused when his hands closed around the hilt and blood started bubbling out his mouth.

"My queen. Why?" he asked.

That was the last thing he was able to say before Aleksei's body gave out and crumpled to the floor. I thought it was over and we should help with the scuffles outside the compound. I woke Rainer up just as Aleksei's dead body started twitching. I was reminded of all those zombie movies Quinn liked so much, but zombies weren't supposed to be real, even among the supes. Supes and humans, once you were dead, you were dead.

I furiously shook Rainer out of his enchanted sleep

stupor as Aleksei's dead body started dragging itself on the floor like some half-squashed bug that refused to die. His eyes met mine, and they were the same dull silver color. Apparently, I killed Aleksei, but Cade's pith hadn't gone to the Underworld.

"I should have known better than to trust another hybrid. You're all vile creatures who should be kept and starved unless I need to make a child I can raise the right way," Cade growled, blood still spurting out his mouth.

His pith was still in Aleksei's body, but he was having trouble controlling it. He was writhing on the floor and trying to get at me. I hadn't heard enough of the initial spell to get Cade's pith out of Aleksei's body. This needed The Order's full attention, especially if there was a witch in the Underworld with this knowledge.

I snapped my fingers, and a Hellfire Cage sprang up around the bleeding body. The dagger was a cherished gift from Jago, but I wasn't about to get it right now. Maybe I'd get it back once Aleksei's body was truly dead.

Rainer and I just stood there, staring at the body in the cage. I realized the rest of the house had gone silent. There were no screams or gunfire anymore. My mates came spilling in with Aria and the rest of hers. They all just stopped and didn't speak when they saw what was in my Hellfire Cage.

"Aria, you bitch," Cade growled. "I should have known you were here and corrupted this hybrid."

"Is that....Cade?" Aria asked, her mouth hanging open.

I looked at my mates. They were all covered in blood, and I didn't want to think about who Jago might have eaten.

"We need to get this thing to Switzerland *now*. I'm

sorry, but victory celebrations and marking are going to have to wait," I said.

"If we're looking at a moving corpse with a blade forged with dragon fire sticking out its chest, I'd say you needed to open that portal five minutes ago, my treasure," Jago said.

I opened a portal to The Order headquarters in the Swiss Alps. If members there were sleeping, they were going to soon find themselves awake.

All my orders came from Xenon, so that was where I brought everyone. There were children in his huge villa, so I had us exit in the woods behind his house. I wasn't about to drop a bleeding, animated corpse in his living room. Xenon would have wards up and sense us. Possession wasn't real and up until now, was mostly a human term, but I was starting to wonder if human possession had been that damned witch in the Underworld and Pith Totems.

It didn't take long for Xenon and his mate, Samara, came running out in their bedclothes. Samara was asking everyone covered in blood if they needed healing and Xenon came over to me. He hadn't looked in my Hellfire Cage yet.

"Are you injured, Liliana? Tell me what happened with the Pith Totem," Xenon demanded.

I pointed to my Hellfire Cage. "*That* happened with the Pith Totem. Cade is animating that corpse, and there's a witch in the Underworld who has a theory on how to get out. If you hadn't found his first Pith Totem,

Cade *would* have escaped the Underworld. You need to send a squad to the highest peak in the Danube Hills in Unseen Moon territory. There's a safe house there that is full of forbidden objects and possibly more Pith Totems. I brought *this* with me because it won't die and I don't know what it is."

"That, my dear, is a Revenant. The spell and theory for it were written by a witch a very long time ago after Pith Totems were forbidden. The idea behind it was so horrible; she was given the final death. The knowledge of this spell used to be limited to the witch who wrote it, a few of her coven members, and The Order."

No one had ever taught me about Revenants before. I was getting angry no one thought to warn me after sending me to destroy a Pith Totem knowing Cade was in the Underworld alive. I was about to snap at Xenon for keeping secrets, but I watched him walk over to the Hellfire Cage. I joined him. If it was possible for Aleksei's dead body to look even worse in ten minutes, it did.

"Let me guess, you got this grand idea from a witch named Rowena, and you promised her a way out of the Underworld?" Xenon sneered.

"Rowena keeps her word, unlike hybrid bitches. It can still work. I'll come up with a plan." It sounded like it was getting more and more difficult for Cade to use Aleksei to speak. Blood was probably starting to clot in his throat. It was all over his face and starting to turn black.

Xenon laughed like he wasn't talking to an animated corpse. I hoped he was laughing because he knew how to kill this body for good.

"Did Rowena explain what happens when you force your pith into another living being?"

"Yes, I become immortal. Even now, that filthy hybrid was unable to kill me."

"You think you'll somehow be able to get your partial pith out of this body and into someone else. It sounds like Rowena didn't explain the details of Revenants to you. Once you start the process of becoming one, you'd better make damned sure you take care of the body you're using. Using a human was foolish. Your greed at wanting to possess a hybrid has proved foolish several times now. You continue to underestimate them."

I sneered down at the corpse. "Do you even know my name, asshole?"

"I don't care what your name is. I hate modern women. You should be more obedient like the Unseen Moon women. An Unseen Moon witch would have been honored to be my queen and not dare lie to a warlock."

Aria finally came to stand by us. "What are we going to do with this misogynist pig? Sending him to the Underworld was clearly too good for him."

"Aria, you haven't met Venus, but she's one of the High Inquisitors, and she trained Liliana. I reached out to one of our best squads, and they've already portalled to the Danube Hills to search for Cade's safehouse. Venus was the one who researched Rowena's Revenant spell and knows how to kill Cade for good."

Now I was angry. Venus trained me for years, and she was hard in her lessons until I mastered something. Venus was a severe teacher, and she always insisted I be prepared for anything and everything. I was about to start asking some serious questions about why Venus didn't come to visit, or I wasn't sent to Venus before I was sent on this mission.

"Oh, don't start your bitching again," I heard behind

me. "I didn't think anyone was actually dumb enough to try Rowena's ridiculous spell and that foul witch has been dead for ages now. Clearly, I underestimated the stupidity of Unseen Moon. How does it feel being trapped in a rotting corpse, you piece of shit? Has rigor mortis set in yet? I've half a mind to leave you in that cage for a few days, but you'd just stink up the place."

Venus was about my height, but rail thin with sharp features and she kept her head shaved. She had a ring through her septum and probably ten piercings in each ear. She was covered in tattoos, but that was what all of The Night Grove Coven did. The tattoos and jewelry were all enchanted for their protection. Venus wanted to put a ring through my nose all through my training, and no matter how much I told her my mother would rip it out with her bare hands, she insisted I would look good with it, and it would protect me.

"Venus, you're going to have to explain Revenants to me when you're done with Cade."

"Really, Liliana?" Venus snapped. "I'll explain Revenants to you *after* you and your mates have marked each other. Five fucking years and you're worried about rare magic that will probably never happen again."

My mates were around me in seconds. Quinn's wolf was out and so was Jago's dragon. "You'll take care how you talk to our mate!" Jago rumbled.

Venus' face finally softened. "I'm talking to your mate like that because I trained the wench for years and I want to see her happy. I can't imagine what all of you went through and The Order failed all of you not figuring it out."

Venus walked over and pulled me into a hug. I didn't

think that witch hugged anyone. "Fine, Liliana. You can watch me deal with the Revenant, and I'll explain what I'm doing, then I demand you go to the penthouse in the main hall, and you and all your mates mark each other to Nature."

"I'd like a little celebration with my mate too," Ronric boomed, pulling Aria into a hug.

Venus looked like she just noticed the seven-foot tall Lycan and the supes surrounding him. "You. We owe you thanks for figuring this mess out. There will be quarters arranged for you in the main hall to celebrate your battle and clean all that blood off you. Did you want to watch too?"

Aria let out a little growl. "You forget, I was betrothed to this ass. I want this over. We'll watch."

"Okay, so get your ass over here, Liliana. Revenant 101. A foreign pith in anyone's body, human or supe, it unnatural. A crime against Nature. The law of order is interrupted. A pith is supposed to move on to either the Underworld or Elysium when the body dies. Rowena's theory was to forcibly remove a pith when death was imminent and shove it into another host. Two piths in one body is against every law of Nature.

"When the host dies, their pith moves on to the appropriate place, but the unnatural pith is trapped. It can't go anywhere because it tried to cheat death. Elysium, Asphodel Meadows, and Tartarus reject the pith as unworthy. It has nowhere to go, so it stays in the corpse."

I was nodding. I understood why I was looking at a talking corpse, but if the entire afterlife rejected them, what were we supposed to do with Cade? He was technically straddling Earth and Tartarus. Even if we could get the part of his pith that was in Aleksei out, we had nowhere to send it to.

"But Cade is still alive in the Underworld and animating a corpse here. I'm not sure how we fix this."

"Easy. Cade already opened the door to the process. Where the hell is Leif?" Venus said, whirling around.

Leif was Venus' apprentice, but he'd been an apprentice for as long as I'd been in The Order and never been promoted. Leif seemed terrified of Venus every time I saw them together. As if summoned, Leif came running from the distance, practically stumbling over his big feet.

He set some huge contraption in front of my Hellfire Cage. It looked like some mechanical wheel, but it was humming with magic. I knew Venus would explain. She always did in great detail whenever she was teaching me something.

"Now, I made this when Revenants were just a theory. I've never had one to test it on. When the wheel spins, it conjures Hellfire in sort of a different way than the cage. I focus it on the Revenant, and it pulls the pith out. If there are multiple Revenants with one pith, it should draw them all out. It should be strong enough to kill Cade to draw his pith here since it had his signature. This Hellfire is a little different than the cage. In theory, it's supposed to burn the pith until it no longer exists."

"That's genius!" I said, eyeing the wheel. "There could be more pith totems coming when they find an Unseen Moon safehouse. Would this wheel work with Rowena? She was able to create a Revenant from the Underworld. Who's to say she won't again?"

"The wheel needs a pith to latch onto, and Rowena can only carry out her plans if she meets a pith in the vast

Underworld who has happened to have created forbidden magic. The chances of her doing this again are rare."

I crossed my arms and glared a Venus. I knew she was shrewd. "You thought the chances of her doing this in the first place was rare, but here we are."

"Let's focus on the problem at hand for now. We need to see if my invention works first. Your intuition has always been an asset, and you're probably right about Rowena. That's a spell that needs more time."

I nodded. "You'll have my help after I resolve my mate situation."

Venus just threw back her head and laughed. "Oh, honey, look at who Nature mated you to. You won't be leaving the penthouse for at least a week."

Venus made me blush like I was twenty-six and her student again. "Let's get the wheel started and see if it works."

"Everyone stand back. Don't touch the wheel until it's finished."

Venus started chanting in the old tongue. The wheel started spinning, and glyphs that had been burned into the wood started burning blue with Hellfire. The entire wheel burst into Hellfire. The Hellfire seemed to direct itself towards Aleksei's body, which started writhing in pain. The noises coming out of the body were just as unnatural as the Revenant. It was shrieking and moaning and looked like it was seizing.

I didn't realize it before, but when I was talking to Cade through Aleksei, he didn't have an aura. Even humans had a distinct aura. I finally saw his aura when it was ripped out his body. It was dingy and tainted. Auras were normally bursting with color. Cade's aura was a gray color I'd never seen before in any living person before.

When it hit the Hellfire in the wheel, it was like someone threw gasoline on it. It was just a pith, but the area we were standing in was starting to reek of burning flesh and hair. There was just a small amount in Aleksei's body, but once the wheel had burnt it out, the ground cracked open.

Cade didn't have a physical body anymore. The pith in Aleksei was gone. I wasn't even sure how this was possible, but in addition to the stench of burning flesh and hair, these horrible shrieks of pain filled the air as the Hellfire destroyed the pith.

I was starting to feel like I was going to vomit. This whole situation of Pith Totems and Revenants was unnatural even without destroying a pith. I was starting to wonder if anyone would think me weak if I left when the flames finally went out. It was over.

Venus turned to me with her arms crossed over her thin chest. "Now, get the hell out of here, Liliana. You did well bringing us our first Revenant and exposing the safe house, but now you need to worry about yourself. The next time I see you, you'd better be marked and mated."

The penthouse in the main hall was meant for royalty The Order was looking to recruit. I probably wouldn't have been set up there even if I hadn't been injured when Xenon brought me to Switzerland. Colnar and Quinn probably hadn't seen it either, but Jago and Cirrus would have. They were both princes of their kind.

It wasn't a long walk, so I wasn't going to open a portal just to get there faster. To be honest, my mind was buzzing with a million thoughts what Cade had turned into, what the squad might find in that safe house, what was going to happen tonight when we did get to the penthouse. They were all vying for attention in my head, and I couldn't concentrate on one long enough to think about it for longer than two minutes.

Cirrus and his naughty little fantasies only had one thing on his mind. He came up behind me and scooped me up, whirling me in a circle. He kissed my neck and set me down. He didn't even seem to notice he got blood all over me. Then, I realized that was probably his intention.

"The penthouse is *perfect* to celebrate this battle like the Fae. And the shower will fit all of us. You're going to love it, Liliana. The victor who won the war is bathed down by the other Fae, then we all fuck every way imaginable. Ever since I drank from that goblet, I know *exactly* how I'm going to mark you."

I swallowed the huge lump in my throat. I was looking forward to the shower, even if it was just taking one alone. The sense of wrongness coming from Cade's Revenant seemed to seep into my pores, and I was sure the smell that came from the wheel when it was burning Cade's pith was enmeshed in these clothes and my hair.

As far as Cirrus' fantasy went, with him, that could mean anything. Cirrus was all Fae and wanted what he wanted, when he wanted it, even if one fantasy didn't make a lick of sense with what he wanted to do next. I always had a ton of fun playing with Cirrus and his various desires, but he'd told me a little of Fae parties. And right now, I had a dragon and a Lycan that thought they wanted to mark me *together,* Cirrus' fantasy, and then I was sure Colnar had something up his sleeve. I was sure someone would be scraping me off the ceiling before everyone was able to mark me.

We were at the lobby of the main hall before I knew it. I was both excited and more nervous than I'd been in a long time. Xenon was busy. Someone was waiting for us to give us the gilded key to the elevator and penthouse. The witch bowed to us and informed us the penthouse had been prepared and food was waiting. She kindly didn't mention any weird magic coming from us, the fact that my mates were covered in blood, and whatever smells remained on us after that wheel did its job.

Quinn pulled me into a hug and got blood on me too

as soon as we were in the elevator. He started kissing my neck now that we were alone. "I've got no idea what the Fae do in the shower after a victory, but I know what *I* want to do to you."

Cirrus just laughed. "Lycan, we don't just bathe the victor. That's where the party starts. What you want to do is totally fine for a Fae victory if it's okay with Liliana."

"Just—I'm nervous about this, okay?" I admitted as Cirrus unlocked the door.

Jago pulled me into a hug. "Treasure, are you hungry? Do you want to wait?"

There was a full spread of food laid out for us, but now Jago had gotten blood on me too. There was no way I was putting food in my mouth with blood smeared all over my body. The feeling I got from Cade's Revenant was enough to kill any appetite I might have had from a battle. My mates didn't seem to have issues with what was smeared all over them, but Xenon was going to kill us if they got it on anything in this plush, ornate room.

"Shower, now," I ordered.

My mates rushed into the bathroom and were already half naked in the short time it took me to get there. I went to unzip my vest, but Cirrus jumped and ran over to me in a panic.

"No, pet. You won this battle. You got the intel and opened the door for The Order to find more of Unseen Moon's trickery. You fought like a true Fae warrior, and I'm honored to have you as my mate. This is where we celebrate *you*. Tonight it is all about you."

The walk-in shower was huge and would fit all of us comfortably. Jago had already started the water running. Cirrus nodded at Colnar and Quinn and disappeared back into the bedroom. Colnar and Quinn were gentle as they stripped me of my clothes. I had to question how Xenon knew what was going to happen tonight when Cirrus came in with Fae candles.

Fae candles were infused with their magic and could burn for days and melt. Something about the magic also caused them to scent the air stronger than human candles or even witch candles. Witches and warlocks coveted Fae candles when they were willing to trade for magic they didn't have.

Cirrus started setting up candles around the bath-room, and I could smell they were already burning in the bedroom. Cirrus snapped his fingers and the candles lit. The scent of Silver Jasmine and Ylang Ylang filled the air. Aphrodisiacs. How the hell did those candles end up here?

I didn't get a chance to ask. My mind was quickly off it when Quinn started nibbling on my shoulder. Colnar was still kneeling in front of me from pulling my trousers off. He started licking and kissing my stomach. I leaned back into Quinn and just groaned. After years apart, I missed their touch. All of them. My nervousness about tonight was melting away. I knew they would do every-thing they could to make me comfortable and pleasure me.

Cirrus had been a busy fairy, and I had no idea where he had the time to get all these supplies. I realized he had a satchel made from the hide of an animal that only lived in Fae territory and it appeared to be stuffed. He pulled out an ornate silver vial with rubies and emeralds inlaid into it.

"How did you manage to get that?" I asked. He hadn't opened any portals to Fae territory since he'd been back and he didn't bring that bag through the portal. The vial contained sacred Fae oil that was used for celebrations and marking mates. Cirrus told me about it once he knew I was his mate, but I wasn't sure if he'd use it because I wasn't Fae.

Cirrus winked at me. "I've been waiting for this so long, and I can plan and kill humans at the same time. My sister put the bag together, and a Fae Order member brought it here once I knew Xenon was giving us the penthouse. I would have portalled home to get it if we had gone back to the villa. We should get you in the shower so I can properly anoint you like a Fae warrior and my mate."

I let them lead me to the shower. The oil was supposed to act as some conduit that would allow the Fae Illumination to mark piths as mates. I forgot all about the oil when I walked into the shower and saw Jago dripping wet with water beaded on his long dreads. He grinned at me and cocked his finger at me to join him.

This shower was almost the size of a small bedroom with iridescent green and blue tiles. I couldn't even begin to count how many shower heads were spraying water from the walls, but the main shower head Jago was standing under was a porcelain Silver Horned Stag that now only existed in Fae and dragon territory.

The water was a perfect temperature as it hit my skin and Jago pulled me to him. I realized how much I missed all of them when Jago kissed me more passionately than he ever did. I felt Cirrus behind me anointing my back with glyphs with his oil. The anointing felt more like the erotic petting Quinn was fond of. I wasn't ashamed to beg for more when I felt it stop.

Jago turned me around gently, and instead of Cirrus, I

saw Quinn in front of me. Colnar and Cirrus were standing behind him stroking their cocks. Cirrus gave me a gentle smile.

"The Lycan and the dragon had the most kills out of our group," Cirrus said. "They go first."

Quinn knelt in front of me and started kissing my stomach. He looked up at me. "Have I ever told you I love how tall you are? You're the perfect height for us to do so many things to you."

I wasn't about to talk about how self-conscious I used to be about my height. I looked down at Quinn and caressed his cheek. "What do you want to do to me now?"

Quinn's eyes flashed gold, and he let out a little growl. His hand cupped my ass and ran down my thigh to my knee. He pulled my leg over his shoulder, and Jago pulled me to his chest for support. Jago had one arm around my waist, and the other was cupping my breast and pinching my nipple.

I sighed and leaned against Jago's hard chest as Quinn's tongue found my clit. Jago was nibbling on my neck. To think, I had been scared of this. The hot spray of all the jets had long washed away any sign of battle from my mates. Cirrus' candles gave the room a heady scent and the oil he had painted into my back had my magic humming.

Quinn lifted my other leg and draped it over his shoulder. His hands were supporting my buttocks and massaging them as he lapped at my clit. Jago helped him hold me up and was leaving little love bites all over my neck and shoulder. He never broke the skin to mark me, but his little nips were turning me on.

Quinn looked up and winked at me. "A little help, Jago?"

Jago's arm tightened around my waist as he supported more of my weight. Jago could have easily paraded around the room holding me in one arm, and he easily held me up without breaking his hold on my nipple or his little bites on my neck.

Quinn's tongue sped up, and I felt two of his fingers slide inside me. I kept my eyes open and greedily watched Cirrus and Colnar stroke their cocks as they took in the scene before them. It had been so long since I had been with any of them or felt any type of sexual urge, I didn't last long to Quinn's fingers and tongue. I shrieked and panted until they finally released me.

Cirrus immediately stepped forward with another vial and four loofahs. I gasped. If that vial was what I thought it was, it was coveted by nearly every supe species and rarely ever acquired. Cirrus just gave me another wink.

"Imp Lotus bath oil is a perk of having a Fae mate, and we just *cannot* bathe the victor without it. This is only the beginning, Liliana."

Cirrus passed the oil around, and they all started to rub the oil into my skin gently. I was starting to think the Fae had the right idea with how to celebrate victories.

PRESENT DAY

To say I owed Cirrus' sister a debt for putting that bag together for him was an understatement. Several herbs and flowers only grew in Fae territory they made toiletries and food with that were highly coveted in the supe kingdom. The Fae being the Fae pretty much kept those things to themselves unless you had something they *really* wanted and couldn't get themselves. That situation was pretty rare and almost never happened, but it didn't stop people from trying to barter strong magic or blood oaths for simple bath oil.

I was starting to see what the fuss was all about. I was scrubbed down and massaged with Imp Lotus bath oil, and Cirrus used his Illumination while washing my hair with Fire Fig shampoo. Something about both the bath oil and the shampoo had my magic humming and my body extra sensitive. Cirrus was on his knees toweling my feet off while Colnar took my hair and Quinn was drying off my body. Jago just stood there looking sexy dripping wet and stroking his erection.

"Cirrus?" I managed to squeak out. All this attention

had me desperate to get them all in the bedroom. "Does everyone react this way to your Fae oils and shampoos and that's why everyone covets them so badly?"

Cirrus grinned up at me and planted a kiss on my thigh. "Not *exactly* this way. You were anointed with Fae ceremonial oil before you used it. You're experiencing Fae magic. Part of me marking you. It's pretty elaborate when Fae's mark their mate, but I think I'm going to have so much more fun because there's five of us. I want to go last. I want to watch you with the others then I know *exactly* how I want to play tonight."

There was something glinting in Cirrus' eyes. Something naughty like he was going to shock all of us tonight. With him, that could be almost anything, and I knew whatever he was up to, he would announce it with a flourish like a Fae prince and then make it happen. I was up for whatever he was plotting because Cirrus' fantasies were always fun and the Fae magic I was experiencing right now had melted all my nervousness away.

Quinn growled. Before I knew it, he had me thrown over his shoulder and was racing to the bed with me. We both bounced on the bed together, and he buried his face in my neck.

"The fairy may want to wait, but I don't think I can anymore."

"You'll have to wait a few more minutes, Quinn," Cirrus said. He had the sacred oil in his hands, and I had no idea what else he intended to do with it.

"We're a different mix than Aria and her mates, so there are additional steps we need to take. The Fae don't deal in blood at all. We can't sense it, and we don't do blood magic. I still don't know why Liliana's bite affects me the way it does. Rainer explained we have sort of a vampire blood bond and that is why we don't want to kill each other anymore. It works on me, and I don't want to kill all of you, but other Fae won't be able to sense it. If we all go into Fae territory, they will try to tear all of you apart for being mated to Liliana at the same time as me."

I didn't understand any of that. Cirrus got drunk and extremely aroused every time I bit him. He begged me to bite him quite often. I wasn't sure how my bite affected him like that, and the goblet bonded him with the rest of them if blood magic didn't work on Fae.

"Just give us the answer, fairy. It's starting to hurt, and my wolf has been waiting to mark Liliana for a long time," Quinn growled.

Even Jago, who was the oldest out of all of us looked put out with Cirrus. "Get on with it."

"I just need to anoint all of you with the sacred oil, so the rest of the Fae know. It won't take long. I can do Quinn and Jago first since you said you wanted to do this together and I'll do Colnar while you're at it."

I knew this needed to happen now that it was explained to me. I had been petrified when Quinn and Jago said they wanted to mark me together, but now I wanted Cirrus to hurry the fuck up. The Fae magic I was feeling was how I imagined Cirrus felt when I bit him.

Cirrus had finished anointing Quinn's back. Quinn growled and dove straight into my breasts and started nibbling and sucking. Jago's dragon started rumbling as soon as Cirrus started rubbing symbols in oil on his back.

Cirrus had hardly finished when Jago was rumbling so loudly the paintings on the walls were shaking. "Liliana Kashini, I acknowledge you to Nature and the Nydred Clan as my mate from this day forward, from now until I perish."

I felt something snap in place inside me. I didn't even have time to think about what just happened because Jago jumped into bed too and started nipping at my ears.

"Do you know how hard it was not to say those words when I was alone with you? It's like a huge burden has been lifted to say them now. I want marking you to be special."

Quinn bit down on my nipple. "Between the two of us, it will be. I didn't think it was possible, but that fairy oil has me harder than a rock."

I giggled and pulled Quinn's long hair. He loved having his hair pulled and played with. I reached behind me and started stroking Jago's cock. "I think the Fae magic is affecting all of us."

Jago broke into that deep-chested laughter I loved so much. "Let it be known that tonight, I said the Fae are actually good for something besides fighting."

"Jago," I warned, giving his cock a little squeeze.

"Playful banter, Liliana. Cirrus and I used to like insulting each other over cards when we were on guard duty. Now, let us continue what we started in the shower because my dragon wants to mark you now more than ever."

Quinn was still going crazy giving me love bites all over my breasts, and I had Jago's huge cock in my hands.

"Well, you both had some grand idea to do this together. We're all here in bed naked. What was your fantasy?"

"Lycan, do you mind if I take the lead for a bit?"

Quinn's reply was muffled because his face was still buried in my breasts, but I think he said it was okay. I didn't think Quinn would ever move, but he got up and leaned against the pillows when Jago asked him to. I looked at Quinn sprawled out on the pillows. His erection was straining against his stomach, and I didn't need either of them to tell me what to do.

I crawled up Quinn's body until I was right where I needed to be. I swirled the head of Quinn's cock with my tongue. Quinn hissed and tangled his hands in my hair. I still wasn't used to having more than one man in my bed at once. I was so focused on Quinn's cock in my mouth, and I didn't notice Jago moving behind me.

I jumped when I felt Jago's fingers brush my clit and his tongue on my ass. None of my lovers had gone there before, but Aria had explained in pretty graphic detail how Kalon and Rainer marked her. I already knew what Jago was doing. According to Aria, as long as they took care in prepping me, I was in for a hell of a time if they did that and apparently, it was Aria's new favorite thing.

Cirrus apparently had an oil for that too because when Jago's fingers replaced his tongue, I knew that was no ordinary lube. Jago was still gentle and trying not to hurt me. Between all the Fae oils and magic going on, my entire body was singing, and I was getting greedy. I took Quinn out my mouth and craned my head back at Jago.

"More," I ordered. I just expected him to do it and went back to sucking on Quinn's cock.

I heard Jago chuckle that I was giving him orders, but he did what I asked. His fingers kept their slow circles on my clit, and he slowly worked another finger into my ass. I moaned all over Quinn's dick. He felt it and thrust into my mouth a little. I started sucking him a little harder and squeezed his shaft with my hand.

Jago let me get used to his fingers, then started thrusting them into my ass. His fingers on my clit sped up. Quinn was growling and pulling my hair. I nearly screamed when Jago stopped what he was doing to me and patted me on the ass. Quinn complained too when I stopped my attention on his cock to turn to ask Jago what he was up to.

Jago was sitting back on his heels just grinning at me like he knew what he was doing to me. "I don't want to wear you out, Liliana, and I don't think I can wait any longer to mark you. And with all this Fae magic going on after all the marking is done, I intend to have you several more times before you fall asleep."

Before Cirrus started with his oils, that probably would have scared the shit out of me thinking I couldn't handle all of them. Instead, I was bold and ready for anything they were going to give me tonight. I didn't wait for Quinn or Jago to tell me how they wanted to mark me. I was part witch, and I had to mark them too. It went both ways with witches, and I wasn't about to lie there being passive while they did all the marking.

Jago decided to torture me, so it was time for a little payback. I knew exactly how I was going to mark my dragon and show him what happened when you crossed a hybrid. Jago looked like he was about to take control, but I shoved him back, so he was sitting again. I grabbed his cock and started stroking it as I kissed him deeply.

Jago was putty in my hands as I pricked his tongue with my fang and let my essence flow into his cock, marking him as my mate. Jago was moaning, and his dragon was rumbling louder than he ever had before. I released him after I'd marked him. His eyes flashed green and gold when his dragon came out to play.

His eyes roamed my body, and he chuckled. "I'm sorry, Liliana. What does my little hybrid prefer to do tonight?"

"Your idea what a good one," I grinned, turning to Quinn.

I slowly climbed Quinn's body and slid down his cock. I had to take a minute just to enjoy the feeling of him stretching me. I let out a contented sigh, and my gaze never left Quinn's gold eyes. Quinn was squirming and had a death grip on my hips.

"You need to mark me too, yes? Please, Liliana!" Quinn begged. Quinn had asked a lot of questions about how the marking would go if it were him while we were together and already knew it wouldn't just be him biting me.

I pressed myself against Quinn and kissed him. Quinn clutched my back and devoured my mouth as I bit his tongue too. I had my hand between us over his heart and sent my essence into him. Quinn's back arched, and he bit my tongue right back, just not enough to draw blood like I had.

I stayed pressed against Quinn. This was the perfect position for him to mark me and I could bite him too. But we were missing something, and Jago was now waiting for permission like a tame dragon. I didn't want a tame dragon. I wanted the Jago back that would just flip me on all fours and take me that way because he wanted it.

"Jago, you're behaving a bit too much," I called over my shoulder.

Jago just rumbled in response. "The safe word is *fire,* my hybrid. If we go too far, say the safe word."

"Jago, get over here and mark me, damn it."

I heard a groan that was n't in bed with us. That was Cirrus' groan. "I love it when you boss us around. If you were back in your battle leathers with a whip telling Jago and Quinn what to do, that would be sexy as hell."

Quinn growled, and Jago rumbled. "You said you wanted to go last, fairy," Quinn grumbled, squirming underneath me. "Butt out."

I felt Jago grab my hips and move behind me. "Play with that boner you can't keep under control and don't say another word. Are you ready, Liliana?"

"Since when you do ask permission, Jago?" Did he expect me to beg?

That was all Jago needed. I could tell he was holding back. His dragon was shaking the walls. He was gentle as he pressed into my ass slowly. Between the Fae lube and Jago's fingers, it wasn't painful like I had imagined. Jago was helping by taking his time. Even Quinn was being patient. He was buried inside me and not demanding Jago hurry up. I had my face in Quinn's neck giving him little nips.

Finally, I had all of Jago. I felt stuffed, but it was an amazing feeling. They were both hitting spots I had no idea existed, and neither of them had started moving yet. I couldn't stand their stillness or fear they were going to break me. I bit Quinn's shoulder and started licking his blood. I ground against Quinn and started thrusting back against Jago.

Quinn wrapped his arms around my waist to pull me even closer to him and started thrusting into me. He buried his face in my shoulder and was growling profanities. Jago had adjusted himself so that he was pressed against my back and could mark me too. I was sandwiched between the two of them having the time of my life.

I would have thought Quinn wouldn't be able to

move underneath me, but he was thrusting into me fast and hard. His pelvis was slamming into my clit and sending jolts through my body. His ability to speak had finally come back. He wasn't just grunting *mine* anymore. He was nipping at my neck, begging me to bite him, and telling me how much he loved me.

I couldn't sink my fangs in and drink without hurting him because my men had stamina. Instead, I left little nips on his shoulder and lapped at his blood. It was almost too much for me. Cirrus' Fae magic amplified everything I was feeling, and Jago and Quinn's cock were thrusting into me at a frenzied pace. Quinn's blood was just the cherry on top.

I could feel my orgasm barreling towards me. I didn't have much room to move, but I was struggling to get as much of Jago and Quinn's cocks in me as I could. My vision went white, and I sank my fangs into Quinn's shoulder as the biggest orgasm of my life overtook me.

It set Quinn off. He howled and sank his canines in my shoulder as he came. My screams were muffled as I sloppily drank his blood. I heard the sound of glass breaking when Jago's dragon roared and I felt his teeth in my other shoulder. I was shuddering and bucking between them thinking my orgasm would never end.

When I finally came to my senses, Jago rolled us over, so he was spooning my back. Quinn craned his head to look over my shoulder, then scooted over to bury his face in my neck. I heard Quinn break into this hysterical laughter.

"Jago, I think Xenon would have made us do this in a shack in the forest if he knew what your dragon was going to do to all the glass and paintings on the wall," Quinn said when he finally caught his breath.

I was still smashed between them, and even if I could get up to see what the damage was, I was too content to move and didn't want to.

Now Jago was laughing. "That's because Xenon is an idiot and didn't realize what was in front of him when a woman like Liliana had his favor. We'll have to have some extra construction done on any villa we end up at because my dragon really liked what just happened and wants to do it again."

"So does the hybrid," I purred, grinding against him.

I heard two more laughs across the room — Cirrus and Colnar.

"Is the hybrid up for playing with an Incubus?" Colnar chuckled.

PRESENT DAY

Quinn and Jago planted a few parting kisses on my forehead and neck before leaving me. There weren't any fights that Colnar was joining me in bed. Quinn and Jago were already hard again and just took a seat to watch the show. Colnar stood at the side of the bed with a plush towel wrapped around his hips. His familiar smirk was back.

"Did you want another playmate to join us, Liliana?"

I knew he was asking because he just watched and listened to me screaming enjoying that, but I knew that wasn't what he wanted. Colnar fed off sexual energy, but when we were alone together, he loved just touching and talking. Colnar probably would eventually want to play with the others, but something as special as marking each other needed to be just us for him.

I leaned forward and ran my finger under the waistband of his towel. I gave him a gentle smile. "Just you, Colnar, unless *you* wanted someone with us." Colnar looked relieved, but he hadn't joined me in bed yet. He looked pretty unsure of himself for an Incubus. I knew how long he'd waited for this and wanted it. "How did you imagine this?"

Colnar's face finally relaxed, and he laughed. "Candles, but not Fae candles and all this Fae magic. Cirrus has a few tricks up his sleeve, and I think he's got some ideas in his Fae head for later he's going to have to run by you. I think you know how I want to do this."

I grinned at him. I should have known he'd want his favorite for this. I let my magic go to my fingertip and let it trace the trail of hair that started from his belly button and disappeared down his towel. Colnar's eyes started glowing violet as I grabbed his towel and pulled him closer to the bed. I pulled myself to my knees and gently took his face in my hands to kiss him.

Colnar and a wave of sexual energy pushed me on my back. Maybe it was the Fae magic in the air tonight, but the violet energy coming off Colnar was stronger tonight, and it almost seemed like I could feel it differently this time. Another wave came at me as Colnar kissed my neck and my eyes rolled back in my head. Was this what Colnar and Aria felt every time?

"Colnar?" I gasped, arching my back and digging my fingernails in his back.

He pulled away, and that smirk on his rugged face was back. "That Succubus from the dungeon that was sent to me? We didn't just watch human entertainment and talk about her love of humanity. She was as old as I am and turned to humans after tiring of supes. I asked her if she knew anything about witches and warlocks being able to see sexual energy like us, but you can't feel it. She had a warlock lover for a little while, and they experimented. It only works on witches and warlocks, but there's a trick to make you feel it like I do. I shared it with Aria in private."

I'd felt it a little, but never like this. I thought I knew what Colnar wanted, but my Incubus had some tricks up his sleeve. Colnar kept it reined in as he covered my body in kisses. It felt like a gentle breeze caressing my skin that kept making me break into goosebumps. Colnar liked to kiss every inch of my body before we got started. He didn't want me to touch him while he was kissing me. That was for later.

Colnar kissed his way back up to my mouth, then flipped me over, so I was on top of him. I knew he would want it to be a little more romantic than what I did with Jago when I marked him as my mate. Colnar was an Incubus and fed off sex, but what he really wanted was love. I think out of all of my mates, he was the only one who disliked his nature a little. The other three flaunted it.

I slid myself into the nook of his arm. It seemed appropriate to mark Colnar by doing something he had been unable to do until he met me. Well, and the Succubus he had to feed on when I sent him away, but I couldn't be jealous about that. I snuggled my face into his chest, and he tightened his arm around me.

I placed my hand over his heart, and it was racing. Was he nervous or excited? I wasn't looking anywhere except his face. His eyes weren't glowing violet anymore. They were their normal inky black. His smirk was gone, and I thought he was actually nervous about this. Like somehow, all of this, everything we had gone through, was somehow going to be taken away from him at the last moment and this wasn't going to work.

I let my essence flow directly into Colnar's heart.

Everyone here had enhanced hearing and would hear if I tried to whisper. This needed to be between Colnar and me, even if all five of us were mates. I reached out to him telepathically.

"I mark you as my mate, Colnar. Until my death, we will forever be as Nature chose us to be."

"Thank you, Liliana. I don't have fancy words to mark you as an Incubus. Just my nature."

"Colnar, I don't hold that against you. I don't think you're going to be unfaithful just because you're an Incubus. I don't judge you. I rather like how you make me feel."

"But I was unfaithful. The Succubus—"

"Was necessary. I drank Xenon's blood, and it felt like cheating every time he forced it down my throat. We all did things to survive while we sorted this. I'm not angry with you."

"I'm being stupid. I've just been so paranoid that since you aren't a Succubus, you'd hate being mated to an Incubus."

I kissed his cheek. "I actually love it. And I love you," I said for everyone to hear.

Colnar's eyes glowed violet. My confident Incubus was back. We'd had this conversation before, but not since he had to feed from someone else and he needed to know I didn't hold that against him. I had this deep feeling of guilt in my gut every time Xenon showed up to give me his blood because of my previous feelings for him, and none of my mates judged me for it. I think Colnar knew deep down I wouldn't, but he needed to hear me say it.

Colnar's thumb traced my lower lip. "I stressed about this so much, but I fantasized how it would play out too."

I bit his thumb. "Stop stressing. I've marked you. Bring your fantasy out and mark me."

Colnar grinned at me. "Well, it's a fantasy you've already brought to life. It's just my favorite."

I climbed out his arms and straddled his waist. I kissed him and bit his bottom lip, sucking his blood. Colnar must not have wanted to overwhelm me with his new trick with sexual energy. It was like this slow, steady stream that called to me like I was parched for it. I needed Colnar right that minute.

I practically pounced on his cock when I mounted him. He sat up, tangled his hands in my hair, and pulled. This was Colnar's favorite position, and now that I thought about it as I rode Colnar's cock, this was my favorite with him too. He always pulled my hair and muffled his cries in my neck. I found I liked the feel of his hands in my hair pulling it because I was making him feel good. I loved the sting of it.

I wore my hair long. It was straight and black and fell past my waist. Colnar could have his hands in my hair and on any part of my back. With his thick cock inside me, I loved his hands wherever they chose to rest.

I became wild, riding him harder as he let the flow of sexual energy grow stronger as he sent it to me. I felt something extra coming from him. Colnar had kept how he would mark me this huge secret. I knew it was because he thought this day would never happen. I didn't know how it worked with an Incubus, but it felt sort like he was marking me as I had marked him.

This was something more than sexual energy, but it didn't feel like an essence either. It was deeper than that. I didn't have time to think about it because Colnar broke out the big guns with the sexual energy he was sending me. I threw back my head and let out a primal shriek.

I sank my fangs in Colnar's neck right as I orgasmed.

Wave after wave of pleasure overtook me until I came down and realized Colnar wasn't done yet. He picked me up and placed me on my back. This was new. We hadn't done this before. He usually finished around the same time I did.

He rested his elbows on either side of my face. His eyes were glowing an intense shade of violet as he stared down into my eyes. He winked at me.

"Wrap your legs around my waist and hold on tight, beloved. Bite me again at the end and make it sting a little."

There was my arrogant, smirking Incubus. And he wasn't joking about holding on tight either. The entire bed was shaking with the force of his thrusts. Between him making love to me that hard and the sexual energy he was sending at me, I don't think I had a coherent thought. All I could do was dig my nails in his back, hang on for dear life, and scream his name.

When I felt another orgasm building, I could tell Colnar was close. When mine hit, and I bit his neck, Colnar just sort of exploded. He let out this huge roar, and I could feel him come, but his sexual energy blasted out away from the two of us.

When the swirling purple cloud stopped, Colnar buried his face in my neck and just started laughing.

"I think that hit Cirrus and reinforced his little fantasy about how he wants to do this. I can do it for some reason, but only if you're okay with it."

I turned my head to look at Cirrus. He was leaning back on an overstuffed chair totally nude, stroking his cock, with this wicked grin on his face now that it was his turn.

With Cirrus, how he wanted to do this could be

anything. When Cirrus had the slightest whim, he made it happen. He'd apparently discussed this with Colnar telepathically while I was otherwise engaged and Colnar was up for it if I was.

What was my naughty Fae prince up to tonight?

Cirrus lazily stood and took his time walking over to the bed. Colnar was still with me snuggled into my chest.

"I won't if you say no," Colnar whispered.

I cocked an eyebrow at Cirrus. "What exactly do you have planned, Cirrus?"

"I'm Fae, and we are celebrating this like a Fae battle. I want to mark you like this is a real Fae party."

"Like Jago and Quinn did?"

Cirrus threw back his head and seemed to find that hilarious. "Sometimes, you say the most innocent things, pet. No, I'll be taking you, and Colnar will be taking me. Jago and Quinn are too narrow-minded ever to have experimented with that to know how amazing it feels. I asked Colnar about it while you were with Quinn and Jago. Between the blood bond and the Fae bond, he can get it up to do that, but only with your permission and if you're okay with it."

I had to think about that for a minute. Would I get jealous and act how my mates had acted before we figured this mess out? This seemed to mean a lot to Cirrus, and this was apparently how the Fae did things. My only experience with this was tonight, but I thought about everything I felt when I was with Jago and Quinn. Cirrus' fantasy was intriguing to me. Feelings of jealousy weren't stirring at all.

"Does it feel like how it felt with Jago and Quinn?"

Cirrus threw back his head and laughed. "Oh, pet, different anatomy, but it feels just as good."

Cirrus was teasing me, and it was time to teach my fairy a little lesson. He seemed to be forgetting I knew about his vulnerable spot. I pounced and yanked him into bed with Colnar and me. I pinned him down and started running my tongue along the point of his ear.

"Mercy, pet, I was just having a little fun. A little to the left."

"Colnar, are *you* okay with this?" I asked, remembering what happened when I sent him away.

Colnar just gave me this grin like he knew the same secret Cirrus did that I didn't. "Yes. The various bonds we have make me able to do this to Cirrus because it means more pleasure for *you*."

"I can draw you a diagram, pet, or we can just show you."

"Quit teasing me, Cirrus," I said, swatting at his ass. I had forgotten sometimes Cirrus' mood had taken him in the direction he wanted to be spanked.

"Oh, pet, my ears, and spanking? Did you have your own ideas for how to do this?"

"Cirrus! You're incorrigible!"

"The Fae are a horny, kinky bunch," Jago said from across the room, laughing.

Cirrus just sniffed. "Like you'd ever get invited to a Fae party."

"We're technically having one now, and you've been waiting patiently Cirrus. Do you want to bicker or do you want to do this?"

"Okay," Cirrus said, taking charge. My Fae prince wanted to be a little bossy today, which was something he liked me to do. "Liliana, I want you to fuck Colnar's face so he can show you exactly what I feel when you're licking my ears. And I want you to do those things to my ears again."

Colnar was apparently feeling a little bossy too. I shrieked as he grabbed me and draped me over his face. His arms locked around my thighs and my eyes rolled back in my head as I felt his tongue on my clit. I felt Cirrus' hand on my face, and I met his green eyes.

"Yes, pet. That's how you make me feel."

"Bring me those ears, Cirrus."

Cirrus groaned and kissed the corner of my mouth all the way to my neck. Licking and sucking Cirrus' ears while Colnar was furious lapping at my clit was a huge turn on. I was grinding myself against Colnar's face, and I may have nipped Cirrus' ears once or twice. Cirrus was enjoying the show and my attention to his ears.

"Yes, Liliana! Fuck his face. Come for us," Cirrus purred, sending his Illumination into my breasts.

I didn't think it was possible for me to come again tonight, but I cried out as it was Cirrus now biting my ears and sending his Illumination through Colnar and me furiously licking my clit. Cirrus wanted to snuggle a little while when he was done. Between Cirrus' Illumination and Colnar's sexual energy, I was quickly becoming a quivering mess even without all the sex I'd had before we'd gotten to this point.

I was riled up again and wanting sex between what the two of them were sending at me. My body started moving of its own accord, grinding against both of them. Cirrus tapped my hip.

"Let us put on a show for you. Colnar will need to prepare me."

I watched Colnar grab the same lube Jago had used on me. Cirrus' eyes were in slits as Colnar worked his ass with his fingers. I really was enjoying the show, but I also really wanted to get involved. I knelt in front of Cirrus and took him in my mouth while Colnar worked his ass. Cirrus pulled my hair and was hissing and moaning.

"Ah, fuck, pet. You're amazing, but I think I'm ready now."

I looked up with his cock still in my mouth and winked at him. I gave it a hard suck as I drew my mouth down his hard length. "How do you want me?"

"On your back on the edge of the bed. Are you ready, pet? You'll be feeling both me and Colnar, both physically and our supe sides."

I kissed my way up to his mouth, then nibbled on his ear. "I think you're trying to kill me, Cirrus."

Cirrus just gave me this evil grin as I lay back on the bed. My Fae prince was in one of his naughty moods, and it was best to just go with it. It didn't matter what Cirrus' mood was; he'd make sure I'd have fun.

He teased my entrance with his cock. "Oh, this is going to be the best Fae party ever. Bite as much as you want. Liliana, you have no idea how much I love you right now," he groaned, sliding into me.

I let out a contented sigh and arched my back. I

thought Cirrus' sacred oil was all we needed, but he practically started glowing with his Illumination. Every inch of his body that touched me was singing. He stayed totally still, and I saw Colnar over his shoulder. Colnar's violet cloud joined the white glow around Cirrus. Cirrus pressed deeper inside me as Colnar's weight was added.

I felt like I was making love to both of them at the same time. Every time Cirrus thrust into me, Colnar was sliding into Colnar. Cirrus would slam deeper into me and grind against my clit. I came almost immediately, biting Cirrus.

Cirrus yelled my name when I bit him and started pounding into me harder. That just set Colnar off. It was like being thrust into twice, and the added grinding of Cirrus' pelvis against my clit was unreal, even without the white and violet lights around us.

"Hold tight, my hybrid. I'm going to mark you now," Cirrus yelled.

I screamed and bucked as all his Illumination flowed into me at once. A screaming orgasm ripped through my body, and I sank my fangs in Cirrus' neck. That was all he needed to go over the edge too. Colnar too. I could tell from the violet cloud. We all came together in a screaming, quivering heap.

We collapsed on the bed together. I was marked by all of them now. I looked over at Jago and Quinn. They were sitting on chairs and quite hard. I had so many ideas for what I wanted to do with my mates tonight. Together, separate, it didn't matter. We were all one now.

And I was feeling quite naughty.

PRESENT DAY

Aria apologized profusely for not calling me right off after they figured out the mate mess because she was wrapped up with her mates. I *totally* got it now. The penthouse was totally trashed. Every mirror and glass was shattered. Porcelain and ceramic antiques were in pieces. Tapestries and paintings had fallen off the wall because Jago's dragon was *really* happy with this arrangement.

When we remembered to eat, Cirrus would open a portal to Fae lands and bring us all sorts of Fae food. I wasn't even thinking about what other people thought we were up to. I took my lovers together and separate. They'd kind of divided up, but it worked. They all liked playing together, but Quinn and Jago liked sharing together, and Cirrus liked Colnar and me to share him. Cirrus also liked me alone, and so did Colnar.

It wasn't weird to share Cirrus with Colnar. It just seemed like a normal part of our relationship since we all got so much pleasure out of it. Quinn and Jago didn't judge, and I'd caught them with their cocks in their hands while Colnar and I were with Cirrus. I didn't think they'd ever join us, but it turned them on.

I didn't even think about how strange it would appear to anyone that we hadn't sent for food until the third day when I heard a commotion outside my door. I could hear Aria and Xenon out there, and I didn't have a stitch of clothing on.

That wasn't something Jago cared about, and he flung the door open naked rumbling about being intruded on.

"I told you it was too soon," Aria snapped.

Xenon pushed his way into the penthouse. He didn't seem shocked at the huge mess in the room.

"Did you forget you have a job to do, Liliana?" Xenon snapped with his hands on his hips like my mother.

I was naked in bed, and I pulled the sheet up to my chin. My mates were all in bed with me except Jago, who was just standing there stark-naked glaring at everyone for interrupting us.

"Can it wait until I'm dressed?" I snapped. "What's going on? I thought you were sending a squad to the safe house. It's only been three days. Have they torn the entire place apart in such a short time? It's in the mountains. How did they even find it so quickly?"

I was rambling because I *loathed* being in trouble. And I didn't really think I should be in trouble. I had valid points. It should have taken days to locate that safe house. They shouldn't need me yet.

Xenon cleared his throat. "Well, between two sets of multiple mates, fairy magic, a Succubus, and Incubus, and a witch and a warlock, all of you caused chaos with your celebrations."

I wanted to get dressed, but I already knew the peace my mates had wouldn't extend to Xenon if I got out of this bed and he saw me naked. Aria, Colnar, Rainer, and Cirrus were laughing like they knew exactly what kind of chaos Xenon was talking about and I was left out again.

Xenon glared at Cirrus. "It's not funny! We told you when you were recruited if you wanted to celebrate like that, keep it contained."

Cirrus just leaned back against the pillows with his hands behind his head. "You all needed to get laid anyway. You're all so stuffy."

Aria was biting her fist trying not to laugh. Rainer snorted, which just set her off. Pretty soon, we were all laughing. Except for Xenon, of course. Some of The Order members were prudes, and the idea of them all having some Fae orgy was too much, and I couldn't stop giggling.

"Are you done?" Xenon snapped. "The squad has been in contact. They are zeroing in on the safehouse and think they are close. They are finding it by an intense sense of wrongness. There is a huge possibility there is a massive safe house in the mountains in Germany full of Pith Totems. We want to pair you up again and send you out as Team Hybrid."

Aria flung her scarlet hair over her shoulder. "I'm up for it, but we need a better name than Team Hybrid. My mates aren't hybrids, and neither are Liliana's."

Xenon shot me this pleading look. "You can come up with whatever name you want. Can all of you leave tomorrow?"

I already knew I could play and work. I already knew I could trust all of my team members. We'd worked well before and I'd always dreamed of working with my idol, Aria. We could handle anything, even a safe house full of Pith Totems.

I exchanged silent looks with everyone in the room. "We can leave tomorrow. We won't let you down."

"Good. And don't think I don't notice what you did to priceless antiques in this room, Liliana," Xenon said, stalking out.

Aria stayed, crossing her arms and grinning at me. "Well, I certainly didn't destroy anything when my mates and I marked each other."

I grinned back. Before, I was a little uncomfortable talking about sex with Aria. I was much more comfortable now. I was marked and mated. I was about to go into the unknown and take on a safe house full of who knew what.

"Jago is responsible for that, but maybe Cirrus will share some of his oils and candles with you."

Cirrus dove into my neck and started giving me love bites. "I'll give you whatever the fuck you want if you just leave. We aren't supposed to leave until tomorrow, and I want more time with my mate."

My mates were all rumbling, growling, or purring their agreement. I wanted as much time alone with them as possible before we went back into danger.

AFTERWORD

The Order of the Red Shadow-Follow along with Liliana's story in book 2 of The Order of the Red Shadow Series, Lethal Shadow, an exciting new paranormal reverse harem romance series from JB Trepagnier. Liliana is known in other circles as Lethal Shadow, a top political operative in The Order of The Red Shadow. Find out how she was bound to her four mates. Now that Aria has told her she's fated to be with all four of them, can she convince them to come back to her? Book 3, The Revenants, Coming soon. Liliana and Aria team up to take on a new threat from Unseen Moon. An evil that has never been seen before—The Revenants. Book 4, The Territory Wars is also coming soon, following Aria's mother and father as they meet and become the first supernatural mates to have a hybrid birth

.

Made in the USA
Middletown, DE
09 May 2023

30309054R00137